A WARMING TREND . . .

At first Nancy had only the sensation of a feathery warmth on her face. She forgot where she was until she took in the springy surface beneath her and the smell of hay.

Then she felt the slow movement of a hand brushing the side of her face, and her eyes flew open.

In a split second, she realized that she was staring at Michael's face, which was suspended only a few inches over her own.

His eyes, soft and brown, were half-closed.

His lips hovered, about to press on hers.

Nancy Drew on Campus™

Available from ARCHWAY Paperbacks

Nancy Drew
on campus™ #25

Snowbound

Carolyn Keene

04296812

AN ARCHWAY PAPERBACK
Published by POCKET BOOKS
New York London Toronto Sydney Tokyo Singapore

AN ARCHWAY PAPERBACK *Original*

An Archway Paperback published by
POCKET BOOKS, a division of Simon & Schuster Inc.
1230 Avenue of the Americas, New York, NY 10020

Copyright © 1998 by Simon & Schuster Inc.
Produced by Mega-Books, Inc.

ISBN: 0-671-00779-3

First Archway Paperback printing January 1998

10 9 8 7 6 5 4 3 2 1

Cover photos by Pat Hill Studio

Printed in the U.S.A.

IL 8+

CHAPTER 1

Nancy Drew had opened her mouth to laugh just as another snowball went *splat* against her face. Through her frosty eyelashes she could see that her attacker was her roommate, Kara Verbeck. As Nancy was recovering, another snow missile flew over her right shoulder. It was launched by Eileen O'Connor, who lived in Nancy's suite of rooms on the third floor of Thayer Hall.

"Die," Nancy called out. In a flash she dropped her book bag into a snowbank, scooped up a chunk of snow, and charged Eileen. She managed to get part of it down Eileen's neck before Eileen saw or heard her coming.

Nancy and her friend George Fayne laughed as Eileen brushed the snow off her dark blond hair.

"This isn't fair," George said. "I want to play, but I've got to get over to Will's to help pack for our ski trip."

1

"We have to get back, too," Kara called out. "We're leaving in one minute."

Nancy waved good-bye to Eileen and Kara as she hurried along through the fresh, deep snow with George.

Wilder University had been buried under two feet of snow the night before, and more was on the way. For now, though, the sky was a bright blue, and the afternoon sun had turned the tired midwinter campus into a sparkling wonderland.

Glistening icicles clung to window ledges and fire escapes, turning dowdy dorms into crystal palaces. Even the benches and trash bins around campus had been transformed into pillowlike snow sculptures.

"It's magic, Nancy," George said. She spread out her arms and spun around. Her short, dark curls flew out from under her ski hat as her long legs high-stepped in place. "Anything can happen when the world is covered in snow—anything."

"Well, then, let it happen," Nancy cried, tossing George's words back at her.

"Okay," George replied. "Then come skiing with us this weekend, Nancy."

"I'd love to," Nancy said, "but—"

"The slopes of White Pass beckon," George urged her. "Will and Andy and Reva really want you to come, too."

"Don't torture me," Nancy protested. Will Blackfeather was George's boyfriend, Andy Rodriguez was his roommate, and Reva Ross was Andy's girlfriend and another of Nancy's suitemates. "I've got mountains of work to plow through, George. No way can I go skiing."

"Headlines?" George asked sympathetically.

"Yep. My personal time-eating machine," Nancy admitted. Recently Nancy had landed a job as co-anchor of the university's cable news show. It was a great job, but on top of her full course load, it meant that she had zero free time.

George's face turned serious. "Nan, you need some downtime, too. Come on. I promise we'll get you back early Sunday."

Nancy walked even more briskly through the icy air. "Michael and I haven't even come up with a lead story for next week's show. We need something better than the snowstorm, and we need to get it together in the next two days."

George's eyes darkened. "And how is Mr. Pushy these days?"

Mr. Pushy was just one of the many nicknames Nancy's friends had given her co-host, Michael Gianelli. Neither he nor Nancy had expected to have to share the anchor job, and from the beginning sparks had flown between them. Michael seemed to do everything possible to scoop Nancy on stories and then take all the credit for the work they did together.

"He's just as maddening as ever," Nancy replied with a sigh. "Good-looking, intelligent, witty—even funny—but infuriating."

"Do you ever think of going back to reporting at the *Wilder Times,* Nan?" George asked. "Is *Headlines* really worth the hassle?"

"Dump my spot on the show, just because Michael Gianelli doesn't want to work with me?" Nancy stopped in the snow and stared at George. "No way," she blurted out. "That's just what he wants."

George held up her hands in defense. "Okay. Okay. Don't get so touchy." Under her breath she muttered, "What about what *you* want?"

"I heard that," Nancy snapped. Then her tone softened. "Sorry," she said, linking her elbow with George's again. "The truth is, *Headlines* is exactly what I want to be doing—even with Michael Gianelli."

"So, you must get something out of working together." George's tone of voice carried a hint of a challenge.

Nancy felt her face get hot. She suddenly felt flustered. "What do you mean?"

"Just what I said," George replied. "You must enjoy something about working with him, or else you'd be back at the newspaper in an instant."

"Yeah, well," Nancy began sheepishly. "He's a challenge. He turns every conversation into a competition." She paused thoughtfully. "But I'm not exactly an innocent bystander. Every time I'm around Michael, I get this uncontrollable urge to squish his big ego. I find myself wanting to one-up him at every turn."

"Well, you two work on camera," George pointed out. "There's chemistry between you on the set."

"Chemistry?"

"Yeah," George said. "At the end of the broadcast, when you talk about your upcoming stories, it looks like you guys are having a blast together." George cast a sidelong look at her friend. "I've heard rumors that you're actually dating Michael Gianelli."

Nancy felt a flash of anger and confusion. She'd heard the same rumors. She bobbed down to grab some snow. She packed it tight and hurled it toward a tree. Bull's-eye.

"That's for Michael Gianelli," she cried triumphantly. "I have to run, George." Nancy began to take the steps two at a time.

"Me, too," George called to her. " 'Bye—and good luck this weekend."

Nancy stopped at the top of the stairs and turned around. "Enjoy the magic."

Nancy was eager to get over to the TV station but decided on a hot, relaxing shower first.

She was about to turn on the water when she heard the bathroom door open and two women walk in. She recognized the voices of Eileen and Kara—and they were talking about her.

"I don't understand," Kara said. "Why *not* tell Nancy about the Money Plane?"

"The last thing the game needs is for Nancy and Michael to decide it's news," Eileen explained.

"But it *is* news," Kara said excitedly. "And the more people who know about it and join, the richer we'll all get. Right?"

Nancy silently raised an eyebrow at what she'd heard. Money Plane? Riches?

Eileen raised her voice over the sound of running tap water. "The university doesn't exactly approve of the Money Plane, which is part of the excitement. It's all very hush-hush."

"Okay," Kara said suddenly. "How do I get in the game, exactly?"

"I don't know *exactly.*" Eileen paused and then continued in a whisper. "There's a meeting tonight where Jean-Marc is going to explain everything. I was told we could join then. Just bring your hundred and fifty dollars and try to think of eight other people you can sign up."

Jean-Marc Chenier was the only Jean-Marc Nancy knew of on campus. He was Holly Thornton's good-looking boyfriend, and Holly Thornton was Eileen's sorority sister.

"I know a few people who joined a couple of weeks ago, and they've already been paid twelve hundred dollars," Eileen told Kara.

"Twelve hundred dollars," Kara said dreamily. "Just tell me when and where."

There was another pause before Nancy heard Eileen say, "Tonight at seven, up on the fifth-floor common area. Be early. It's going to be crowded."

Nancy heard the door open as Kara said, "I can't wait," and then they were gone.

When Nancy was certain she was alone, she turned on the shower and let the hot water pour over her shoulders.

Sounds like a definite story for *Headlines*, she thought. She hoped that Michael Gianelli hadn't heard about it yet. It would be sweet—very sweet—to beat him to it.

"Okay, let's get going," Liz Bader said in a no-nonsense voice. She flipped through the dresses hanging on the rack of the used clothing boutique. When a slim, black velvet gown appeared, she draped it over the arm of her roommate, Ginny Yuen.

Ginny stared at the rhinestone bow on the front. "I know you want me to cut loose and have a little fun. But a full-length gown with rhinestones?"

"Don't be ridiculous," Liz said. "Look *beyond* the dress. You chop it off at the hem. You take off the bow. Voilà. A short, black, sexy dress for fifteen dollars."

Ginny cocked her head and held the dress up for examination. "Mmmm. Maybe you're right."

Liz rushed over to sort through the used handbags. "Of course I'm right."

Ginny shrugged and held the dress up to face the mirror. It looked great—or would. Liz was right. She should get the dress and have a little fun. Ever since she'd broken up with Ray Johansson, she'd spent almost all of her time buried in her pre-med studies and volunteering at Weston Memorial Hospital. She was starting to feel as dry as sawdust inside.

"Work, work, work," Liz chided her roommate

while checking out a big-shouldered sequined jacket. "You're almost as bad as I am, Gin. You've got to cut loose once in a while. You don't want to end up like those uptight doctors who've got wires and computers in their chests instead of hearts."

"You can try the dress on at home if you want," the woman behind the counter said. "Just bring it back if it doesn't work."

Ginny pulled out her wallet as the woman put the dress in a bag. All the while, she watched a movie running in the back of her mind. It starred Ray and his reaction to the dress. She knew he would love it, even—especially—without the alterations.

Ginny felt a pang. Funky, intense, creative Ray. She had felt so alive the months they were together. People had thought that it was strange that they were together—the pre-med student and the lead singer and songwriter in a rock band. No one understood how connected they were.

Still, when Ray began to pressure her to leave her medical studies to focus on their shared passion for writing songs, Ginny pulled away. He didn't seem to understand that she had her own dreams, dreams of being a doctor.

"Come on," Liz said, breaking into Ginny's reverie. "Let's go back to the room and fix the dress. There are a million parties this weekend, and you're going to look amazing in this dress at every one of them."

"Yeah." Ginny laughed. "But we'll probably be snowed in on my one weekend off."

"You may be right," Liz agreed as they stepped outside. The wind whistled along the downtown storefronts, and the sky that had been bright when they entered the store was now blotted out by high, dark clouds. "It feels like more snow is on the way. But then, a blizzard's the perfect backdrop for romance, too."

"Ski boots, two pair. One size eight. One size twelve," George said.

"Check," her boyfriend, Will Blackfeather, replied.

"Lip balm, two sets of thermal underwear, two emergency space blankets."

"Check, check, check. They're on the bed."

"Cash for cross-country permits, gas, food, and motel."

Will's head of dark hair appeared from behind the closet door. His sheepish grin showed his teeth very white against his tawny skin. "Cash?"

George put a hand on her hip and tried to look irritated. Will was the one assigned to money duty for the trip: figuring out a budget and hitting the cash machine *before* they left.

Just then the five o'clock weather report came on the radio, and George broke her pose to lunge for the volume control. "Here's the weather report, Will."

"The National Weather Service has issued a travel advisory for the general Weston area. A major storm front is moving in, and heavy snow, high winds, and dropping temperatures are expected in the early morning hours—especially in southwest Wisconsin and northern Illinois. I repeat . . ."

Frustrated, George turned the volume back down. They had planned to leave that night, before any more storms hit, but Andy's car was in the garage for repairs and wouldn't be ready until the next morning.

"No problem," Will said. "Even if we don't beat the storm, Andy's four-by-four will get us up to Wisconsin."

"It had better." George felt a rush of pessimism take hold. "I've been so psyched to go skiing, I'll just die if we wind up stranded here."

"Lighten up, George," Will said cautiously.

"All I've been doing for weeks is study, study, study," George complained. "My brain is turning to mush, Will. I really need a break. I *need* to go skiing!"

Will tossed a pair of socks into his pack, then took George in his arms. He brushed a stray curl off her forehead. "It's not as though we're going all the way to the Rockies."

George looked at him squarely. "Promise we'll get there?"

Will tugged her close to him and in a slow-motion judo move laid her out gently on the floor. "You worry too much."

"Do not." George hooked an ankle around his

leg and scrambled free. In an instant it was she who had him pinned to the floor.

"Do, too." Will pulled her down and kissed her, sending shivers down to the tips of her toes.

They looked at each other and sighed before wrapping themselves up in another kiss. George suddenly felt all of her tension melt away. This was the man she loved.

"Mmmmm," Will murmured into her ear. "Alone with you for an entire weekend."

"We'll be with Reva and Andy," George reminded him, slipping her fingers through his long hair.

"Not at night," he said, drawing her into a warm embrace. "Are you okay with this?" Will asked in a gentle voice.

"Um, yeah," George replied, though she felt her body tense up. She and Will had slept together months before. They'd promised to stay faithful and always use protection. But after a recent pregnancy scare, George had said, "No more."

At first Will hadn't understood why she'd backed off. She hadn't been pregnant, after all. But he hadn't pressured her, and slowly he'd come to see that their relationship was more important to him than whether or not they were having sex.

"You're going to be pretty hard to resist this weekend," Will murmured, nibbling down the length of her neck.

The sensations George felt made her wonder

if she might not be ready to go back to the way
things had been.

"I am always hard to resist, Will Blackfeather.
Remember that." She took his face in her hands
and guided his lips back to hers.

"Hey, there's Stephanie." Liz pointed her out
as she and Ginny strolled up a snowplowed path
between Rand Hall and the dorms across the
campus lawn.

Ginny recognized their old suitemate Stephanie Baur, tall and cool in black stretch pants,
fur boots, and a sleek white parka with fur trim
that showed off her long dark hair to great
advantage.

Liz cupped her hands over her mouth. "Hey,
Stephanie."

Stephanie hurried up to them, eyeing Ginny's
shopping bag. "Hi. Looks like you've been having fun."

Ginny grinned. "How's Jonathan's business
trip going? Is he calling you every night?"

Stephanie gave Ginny a mild smile. She and
her husband, Berrigan's department store floor
manager Jonathan Bauer, lived in a small off-
campus apartment. But Jonathan was in the middle of a business trip to Chicago, so Stephanie
had returned to her old room in the dorm while
he was away.

"Okay, she's not talking," Liz concluded as
they walked past a group of cross-country skiers.

"There's a big party tonight at the Norwegian

House." Stephanie gestured toward the skiers. "You're supposed to come on skis."

"Fun," Ginny said.

"Yeah," Stephanie went on, "everyone is psyched to party this weekend. The frat houses all have big fireside dances planned. There's a bonfire party over at the lake. And someone in the dorm is talking about a polar bear swim contest."

"Mmmm," Ginny said, suddenly realizing that marriage hadn't changed Stephanie's party-animal personality one bit. "What are you up to this weekend?"

"I don't know," Stephanie said casually. "Little bit of this. Little bit of that."

Ginny found herself staring at Stephanie's confident expression. Even with her husband away, Stephanie acted as self-possessed as ever. She was one of the most independent people Ginny had ever met. She didn't need Jonathan—or any guy—on her arm to have a good time.

And neither do I, Ginny told herself. I've got to get Ray out of my head and toughen up. Being a workaholic hasn't helped me forget him. Maybe pretending I'm Stephanie would work.

CHAPTER 2

The fifth floor of Thayer Hall had a large common area with lots of big sofas and extra folding chairs, but there still wasn't enough room for the Money Plane meeting. Nancy showed up fifteen minutes before the meeting was to start, but already most of the available seats and the floor space in front had begun to fill up.

"Can you believe this?" a frizzy-haired girl on one side of Nancy asked.

"What a zoo," Nancy commented.

Nancy was lucky—she had found a seat next to a guy busily typing on his laptop computer. To her left was the frizzy-haired girl, who was carefully counting a wad of bills tucked inside her purse.

The stuffy air in the packed room was filled with hushed chatter.

Nancy pulled a notebook from her inside jacket pocket. The whole crazy scene had piqued

14

her curiosity. The Money Plane game was looking like promising material for the next *Headlines* broadcast.

Nancy glanced around discreetly. She hoped
that Eileen and Kara, wherever they were in the
crowd, wouldn't spot her.

A portable display board had been set up in
front, where Jean-Marc Chenier stood signaling
for quiet. His dark hair was neatly combed, and
he wore a pressed denim shirt tucked into black
jeans. Nancy could understand why Holly Thornton, or anyone else, would have gone for him.
Not only was he handsome, he gave off an aura
of confidence—definitely the right kind of guy to
trust with money.

"Hi, everyone," Jean-Marc began. He started
passing out photocopied pages of information to
the group. "Thanks for coming."

"Hey," the guy with the laptop computer whispered. "Isn't that your partner from *Headlines*—
Michael Gianelli?"

"What?" Nancy hadn't quite caught what he'd
said.

"I watch your show. You're Nancy Drew, and
that guy in the hat up front is Michael Gianelli."
He winked. "Doing an undercover story?"

Nancy's mouth dropped open.

"I won't say a word." Her neighbor went back
to tapping on his laptop.

Nancy studied the throng of tightly packed
bodies again. There he was, crouched down in

front, only a few feet from where Jean-Marc was standing. Nancy felt a wave of exasperation hit her. Michael was wearing a baseball cap that she recognized all too well. As he turned slowly to look at the crowd, she could see the tiny hole just above the cap's bill. He was wearing a miniature video camera that belonged to the studio. Michael must have gotten permission from Sidney Trenton, the faculty advisor, to film the meeting. He hadn't even mentioned it to her.

As Nancy watched, the camera came to a stop directly on her. Michael had spotted her. He was grinning like a fool, and then, he had the nerve to wink at her.

She had a sudden impulse to climb across the room, snatch his cap, and stomp on it. Fortunately, before she could act on that impulse, Jean-Marc started his speech.

"Tonight, you can call me Flash," he said with a broad smile.

A few people laughed softly, and he held up his hands. "I know it sounds crazy. It's a nickname, of course—a little tradition we have aboard the Money Plane. And now I have a confession to make to you folks. I like to have fun and I like to make money." Jean-Marc shouted out his confession with pleasure. "Are you with me?"

"Yeah," answered the audience.

"I can't hear you," Jean-Marc cried. "Are you *with* me?"

The audience exploded in a raucous cheer of "YEAH!"

Nancy recognized Jean-Marc's technique of getting everyone excited and feeling like a cohesive whole.

"All right, now listen up. The particular investment game I'm organizing tonight is called the Money Plane," Jean-Marc explained. His words quieted everyone down instantly. He was in complete control of the meeting now.

He picked up a wooden pointer and began explaining the large diagram of a pyramid on the display board. The pyramid had fifteen blocks: eight on the bottom, four in the second row up, then two, and one at the top.

"This game is one of our most successful because of its relatively low initial membership fee of a hundred and fifty dollars." Jean-Marc said.

"That's low?" the girl next to Nancy whispered.

"We use airplane seating as a metaphor to help illustrate this particular financial strategy. All you college students know what a metaphor is, don't you?" Jean-Marc paused for polite laughter from his audience.

"At the bottom of the pyramid are eight *passenger* seats," Jean-Marc went on. "You pay your one-fifty to get to sit in one of these seats. In the next row are four *crew* seats."

Jean-Marc looked around to make sure he had the room's attention. "When eight new passengers pay for their seats, you get to move up to the crew section. Half stay on the same plane and half move to another plane. Are you with me?"

"Yeah," the audience shouted.

"The row above the crew seats has two co-pilot seats. What happens when two more sets of new passengers board the Money Plane?" Jean-Marc asked.

The crowd shouted out its answer.

"That's right," Jean-Marc cried. "You move up to the top seat, the pilot's seat. And, friends"—he paused—"that's where you want to be. Because the next eight passengers pay their money to *you!* And then the pilot—that's you—flies away, twelve hundred dollars richer. It's that easy."

"Sounds a little *too* easy to me," Nancy muttered under her breath. "Not to mention that the plane is likely to crash."

"As long as there's a fresh flow of new passengers, everyone eventually gets to the pilot seat and makes twelve hundred dollars." Jean-Marc sounded very reassuring.

"Mathematically, it can't realistically work for every passenger to make it to the pilot seat," the guy with the computer shouted out.

Jean-Marc shrugged and flashed his beautiful smile. "What can I say? It works for me. Today I'm going to be paid twelve hundred dollars."

"Yeah," the crowd shouted, silencing the guy's logical objection.

"Why do you call yourself Flash?" someone else wanted to know.

"That's a good question, but first let me say that this game is a win-win situation for those of us trying to scrape through college. It's pretty foolproof. The problem is—well, the university officials."

Nancy listened carefully. Here it comes, she thought. Get-rich-quick schemes were always too good to be true.

"Wilder University considers investment games such as this to be gambling, and doesn't allow them on campus," Jean-Marc explained over the groans of the audience. He held up his hands for quiet. "I know. I know. Bureaucrats hate it, even though they've never checked it out." He shrugged. "So we use code names. And we pay in cash."

What Nancy understood was that everyone there was stepping into a lot of trouble with the university.

"All right," someone called out. "Here's my cash."

"Let's do it," another cried.

"There are six available passenger lists on the side table," Jean-Marc called out over the swelling noise. "Line up in front of one of them if you want to join," he shouted.

There was a stampede to the side of the room. Nancy moved forward, hoping for a look at the sign-up sheets.

"Nancy?" She heard her roommate Kara's voice next to her. "What are you doing here?"

"I heard about it in the cafeteria. It sounded interesting, so here I am."

Eileen, who was with Kara, asked, "Interesting as an investment, or as a story for *Headlines?*"

"Nancy," Kara whispered, "don't spoil it for the rest of us. We could get in trouble if you expose us."

"I'm just checking it out, Kara, okay?" Nancy more or less lied. "I don't want to get anyone in trouble." This was the truth.

Nancy edged her way up to where she could see two of the sign-up sheets.

The pyramid with the name Flash in the pilot's seat was filling up quickly, and Jean-Marc was taking the passengers' cash. Another pyramid had the name Ace at the top, and a tall, lanky guy was taking the money from those sign-ups.

Nancy studied Ace. He had curly red hair, a narrow, freckled face, and a gray baseball cap. The cap's logo was a bluebird with a black beak. It didn't belong to any team she knew.

"Excuse me, Nancy," she heard Michael's voice behind her. "I need a closer look at those sign-up sheets."

Instead, Nancy grabbed his arm and shoved her way through the waiting "passengers" into the hall.

"Hey, Drew, cool it!" Michael whispered fiercely as they got away from the crowd. "I was filming in there."

"Why didn't you tell me you were coming?" Nancy asked.

Michael's dark eyes seemed to crackle with the

challenge. "Why didn't you tell me *you* were?" he replied.

"I came to check it out. *You* came wired, *intending* to do the story," Nancy answered in a loud whisper. "There's a big difference."

"The only difference," Michael said calmly, "is that I take action. That's why I'm the one actually documenting this meeting. Not you."

Nancy felt frustrated and angry, but she knew Michael had a point. Having the meeting on tape would make a great exclusive, but she was worried about getting the students in that room in trouble.

"Listen, Michael," Nancy said. "Get some more footage, but I'll meet you at the student union later and we'll talk about editing out the innocent players."

"Okay, Nancy, we'll talk," Michael said. "But just which innocent players are you talking about? I think you're confusing innocence with stupidity. And, I wonder, do you have the guts for reporting, after all?"

How dare you, she thought, but she replied calmly. "And I wonder if you have enough integrity for reporting. I'll see you later."

Nancy walked away. As she did, she noticed a yellow sticky memo paper stuck to her shoe. She picked it off and instinctively read it. It was obviously some sort of note to the Money Plane leaders. She quickly stuck it in her pocket to look at someplace other than right outside the meeting.

As she walked across the crunchy snow to the

union, Nancy thought about the investment game. No matter how charming Jean-Marc was, the Money Plane just couldn't keep working. Couldn't the investors figure that out?

"Look at this shot of you in that slinky satin slip," Holly Thornton said, sticking a large, black-and-white photo of Bess into the Kappa sorority scrapbook. "You were an awesome Maggie the Cat."

Bess sat across from Holly at a table in the student union lounge. They were sorting through a folder of *Cat on a Hot Tin Roof* publicity shots and reviews. Bess had run into Holly, and they'd decided to work on the scrapbook together.

Bess remembered how it had felt to be on stage in front of all those people in the audience as Maggie. It had been a personal triumph over stage fright as well as an outstanding first step in the stage career she hoped to have.

"Oh, look at the one of you lounging all over the bed." Holly laughed.

Bess looked, then covered her eyes. "I look so fa—" She stopped herself even before Holly said, "Stop right there."

"I stopped," Bess said with a laugh. Part of her eating disorder therapy was focusing on changing her image of her body, which she had always thought of as fat, fat, fat. She had, in fact, a fantastic figure. She simply wasn't as skinny as a model.

The jukebox blared and there was a steady

stream of students walking by. They came in with bright red faces from the cold, stomping the snow from their boots and shaking it from their hats and gloves.

A number of students called out to Holly about having just seen Jean-Marc, and something that sounded to Bess as if Jean-Marc had been taking bets on some race.

"What is that all about?" Bess asked.

Holly pasted another photo in the book.

"Haven't you heard about the Money Plane?" she asked casually. "It's hot."

Holly knew about any and everything that was hot on campus.

"No, what is it?" Bess shrugged. "I've been out of touch recently."

Holly shrugged in return. "Jean-Marc's really into it. It's a money investment game, and he's made a bundle off it."

"A money investment game? Here at Wilder?" Bess asked. "How do you play?"

"You come up with a hundred and fifty dollars cash," Holly said, leaning forward on the table conspiratorially. "Then you invest it. If enough other people join up, you get twelve hundred dollars."

"Just like that?" Bess asked.

Holly shrugged again. "Jean-Marc's really jazzed about it. There's a lot of interest."

"Sure," Bess said warily. "Everyone needs money. But who's got an extra hundred and fifty dollars to spend on some crazy scheme?"

"Actually, a lot of people do, or at least they come up with it. I guess not everyone thinks it's a crazy scheme. But Jean-Marc didn't have to pay a cent. The game organizers let him in for free for running meetings and rounding up other players."

"I didn't mean to sound judgmental, Holly, I'm sorry," Bess said, screwing the cap back on her glue stick. "But doesn't this game sound a little fishy to you? I mean, how many other players are enough?"

Holly didn't seem content with Bess's apology. "Oh, I don't know, not that many others. What I do know is that Jean-Marc has made money, so I guess everyone else can, too. And I happen to trust my boyfriend."

Just then there was a commotion at the door, and Bess and Holly both turned to see what was going on.

"Wait up, Michael!" she heard Nancy's voice ringing through the room. Several heads turned. Bess cringed.

"Those two," Holly whispered with exasperation. "They are always at it. What are they, in love or something?"

Bess waved, catching Nancy's eye as she and Michael sat down at a corner table. Nancy waved back and simultaneously rolled her eyes, before turning back to Michael.

"Nancy spends an awful lot of time with that guy these days, but she claims that she's not in love," Bess said.

"You're dead wrong, Michael," Bess heard Nancy say loudly.

Bess smiled, remembering that Nancy's last relationship, with Jake Collins, had started out similarly. They had been competing reporters at the *Wilder Times,* and their work relationship had crossed over into something more intimate. Nancy may not know it, Bess thought, but I smell a crush coming on. And I sure know the signs.

"Hey, Holly," a male voice came from a distance. Holly and Bess both turned.

Jean-Marc was winding his way through the tables, carrying a beat-up canvas briefcase. He looked tired.

"Jean-Marc," Holly answered, standing up and grabbing a chair for him.

Jean-Marc collapsed in it and waved his hand weakly at Bess. He pulled off his hat, revealing a head of tousled, thick black hair. Bess had met him at the Kappa House and thought he was completely gorgeous, with his deep-set brown eyes, high cheekbones, and wide shoulders. He was French Canadian, at Wilder on an exchange program, but his accent was very slight. "Hi, you guys. I'm beat."

"How's it flying?" Holly asked him.

Bess wondered whether Holly was making a joke or was too uneasy to ask about the Money Plane openly.

Jean-Marc leaned back and raked his hair with one hand. "It's a zoo. Everyone wants in on the action, but I'm pumped," Jean-Marc said. "We just had a big meeting in Thayer Hall."

"Want some coffee?" Holly asked him.

"Yeah," Jean-Marc said. "I'll go get some." He scanned the room until his gaze landed on Nancy and Michael. "Isn't that your friend Nancy Drew, Bess?"

"Yeah," Bess answered. "But I wouldn't—"

"I'll be back in a minute," Jean-Marc said as he headed toward the *Headlines* hosts. "Nancy seems perfect to be a 'passenger.' "

"Jean-Marc." Holly tried to stop him, but he just gave her a thumbs-up sign as he walked away.

"Oh, no." Bess groaned. "Doesn't he know Nancy has an investigative news show?"

Holly shook her head. "No, Bess, I don't think he does."

"Well, knowing what I do about Michael Gianelli," Bess said grimly, "I bet he'd like nothing better than to blow the lid right off this game and expose everyone involved."

"You're too soft for this business, Nancy," Michael said firmly. "The Money Plane is clearly a rip-off pyramid scheme, and it's a legit story for the show."

Nancy glared at him. "I'm not saying it isn't. But, you've got some of my best friends on camera, conducting business that's against university policy. I just want to edit the piece very carefully so we don't implicate anyone. We have enough tape without hurting the people who are being taken advantage of."

Michael leaned back and crossed his arms over his chest. "Like I said, you're soft. And not particularly objective when it comes to news."

"And you're not particularly ethical when it comes to people's lives," Nancy retorted.

They'd been arguing these same points over and over—just in different words—since they'd sat down.

"Hi, Nancy." Jean-Marc's voice broke into their argument.

Michael looked up at Jean-Marc and wished more than anything that he hadn't taken off his spy-cam baseball cap. He couldn't believe that Jean-Marc was virtually volunteering to be sacrificed.

"Hi, Jean-Marc," Nancy said quietly.

Michael was grinning a triumphant grin as he stood up to shake hands. "Jean-Marc, I'm Michael Gianelli, glad to meet you."

"Pleased to meet you, too," Jean-Marc said, taking a seat. "I saw you both at the Money Plane meeting tonight. But I don't think you signed up, so I thought I'd come over to see if you had any questions about it."

Michael cocked his head and stared at him. "Thanks."

It dawned on Michael that Jean-Marc really had no idea what they were up to. He probably didn't even know they produced *Headlines*. Why, oh why, didn't Michael have his cap on?

"We have a couple of passenger seats left," Jean-Marc said. "It's a great chance to make some quick money. Can you imagine what you'd do with an extra twelve hundred dollars?"

"Sure I can, Jean-Marc," Michael said smoothly. "But then again, what would I have to do to get it?"

"Simply invest a hundred and fifty dollars and round up more passengers for the game," Jean-Marc explained.

"Uh-huh," Michael said, nodding. "And what happens to all of those passengers I round up?"

"They get paid, when they fill enough passenger slots," Jean-Marc said slowly, his eyes beginning to darken. "The game just keeps going."

Michael rubbed his chin, then pulled out his reporter's notebook and pencil. "I'm trying to work out the math here, Jean-Marc. How many people would you say were at the meeting tonight?"

"Easily over one hundred. Say, one hundred and fifty," Jean-Marc said proudly. "You see, it's a very popular investment."

Michael scribbled in his notebook while Nancy looked on with a dazed expression of disbelief.

"Taking notes?" Jean-Marc asked.

"Yeah," Michael said. "We're thinking about doing a story on this investment scheme for a show we do called *Headlines*."

An angry red began creeping up the sides of Jean-Marc's face.

Michael continued. "You'd need thousands of

new passengers to promote everyone to pilot who was at tonight's meeting and pay them. Have you ever thought about that?"

"Oh, great," Jean-Marc snapped. He stared fiercely, first at Michael, then at Nancy. "I thought I made it pretty clear that I have to keep a low profile. The game needs a low profile." He stood up abruptly. "What I don't need is your so-called investigative reporting."

"But, Jean-Marc, we really want to know more about the game," Nancy pleaded.

"Good try, Nancy," Jean-Marc said accusingly. "If you were really interested, you would have asked me back at Thayer Hall. It's pretty clear you're just digging up dirt for your tabloid TV show."

"May I quote you?" Michael asked with a smile.

Jean-Marc turned and stormed off, and Nancy instantly turned on Michael.

"Great, Michael," she said sarcastically. "Really outstanding journalism."

"What?" Michael asked with mock astonishment. "I thought you'd like the honest approach. I just came right out and told him the truth, that's all."

"Don't fool yourself," Nancy cautioned as she stood up and gathered her belongings. "The only approach you're interested in is stirring up trouble. I can't deal with you now. I have work to do."

Nancy rushed out of the lounge and out of the building before even putting her coat on.

As Michael watched her strawberry blond hair gently bounce away, he felt an odd urge. He suddenly wanted to chase after Nancy—and apologize.

CHAPTER 3

The Friday night parties were in full swing, and so was Stephanie. The band, Blur My Vision, had cranked up the volume until the walls of the Cave were vibrating. Lights sparkled from the ceiling. Laughter bubbled up in between sets.

It seemed to Stephanie that half the student body had crashed her favorite underground campus hangout, and Stephanie loved it. She was dancing with a tall, sexy guy who had a blond ponytail. Before that her partner had been the South African exchange student who sat next to her in Western Civ.

Nothing like a huge snowfall to put everyone in an intense party mood, Stephanie thought. From the looks of the snow-encrusted partygoers who were squeezing into the room, the snow was not letting up.

"You go, girl!" Liz cried out to Stephanie over the din. She and her boyfriend, Daniel Frederick, were perched together on a table, swaying to the music. "What's it like to be a free woman?"

Stephanie rolled her eyes and let her partner spin her away from Liz's proximity. Ever since her temporary move back into the dorms, everyone had been asking her the same thing: Where's Jonathan? How's Jonathan? Have you heard from Jonathan?

To escape thinking about Jonathan, Stephanie danced and danced and danced, throwing her long black hair back and forth until she was dizzy but satisfied that every male in the near vicinity was staring at her.

"Whoa, Ginny. Don't you look hot!" Stephanie heard someone yell.

Stephanie tried to turn around on the jammed dance floor to get a peek at Ginny, but she was blocked by a bear of a guy wearing a giant moose-antler hat.

When the music finally broke, Stephanie made her way back to Liz and Daniel. She felt desperately thirsty and was still reeling.

"All right!" Liz shouted, scooting over on the table to make room for Stephanie.

"Sorry I mentioned your freedom from Jonathan," Liz shouted into her ear with a good-natured nudge. "Must be a sensitive subject."

Stephanie shrugged. Why should she have to answer a whole lot of personal questions, just because she happened to be married and her husband was out of town?

"Hi, guys!" she heard Ginny call out. She was

weaving her way through the crowd in a clingy black dress. Her straight dark hair shimmered on her shoulders.

"Hey," Daniel called out, pushing his tortoise-shell glasses up on his nose. "What did you do to yourself, Ginny? This is not the Ginny I remember."

Ginny flushed and squeezed in next to Daniel.

"It's the dress, Daniel," Liz said, scolding him. "Open your eyes."

Daniel rubbed his eyes and pretended to look shocked.

Stephanie laughed and took a sip of her drink without once shifting her gaze from the crowd. Her focus suddenly sharpened.

A guy with dark curly hair and a black leather jacket strolled out of the crowd and gave Daniel a friendly punch on the arm. He had a slightly rumpled, relaxed way about him, and Stephanie couldn't take her eyes off him.

"Ginny, this is my buddy Ricky Perelis," Stephanie heard Daniel shout over the noise. "Ricky, Ginny Yuen."

Stephanie checked out Ginny's short black dress, which had transformed her skinny pre-med look into something that even Stephanie had to admit was more than halfway alluring.

At the same time, Stephanie kept her eye on Ricky, who dragged a chair over next to Ginny and started talking to her.

Ginny's face brightened and she threw back her head to laugh.

The music started up again, but Stephanie didn't move toward the dance floor. She watched as Ginny gave Ricky a teasing little punch in the arm. How? Stephanie wondered. How could bookworm Ginny snag some of the cutest guys on campus? First there was that hot songwriter, Ray Johansson. Now this!

"I'm Stephanie, by the way," she interrupted, reaching in front of Ginny to place her hand lightly on Ricky's chest.

"Hi, Stephanie. Ricky here." He took her hand and shook it. "Nice to meet you."

"Ricky's an archie, like us," Liz explained. "His head is full of weird stuff about reinforced concrete, roof pitches, measure drawings . . ."

"Rich clients," Stephanie teased, winking at Ricky.

Ricky's glance dropped down the length of Stephanie's jumpsuit, and she felt a tiny thrill. "No," he said, smiling. "Keep those big money types away from me. I'm into public landscapes."

"Parks and monuments," Liz filled her in. "He's definitely not the big-corporate-office-building-type architect, are you, Ricky?"

"Mmmm. But I bet you'll give in one of these days," Stephanie said, to tease him.

"Maybe I will," Ricky replied, a little taken aback. "But I hope not."

Stephanie kept her eyes on him as she arched her back ever so slightly. It was amazing how well her flirting muscles still worked after all these weeks of marriage.

"I'm working on a design for a war memorial right now," Ricky went on. "I was really inspired by what Maya Lin did with the Vietnam memorial in D.C. There are some really fine rock quarries in this area, and I'm going to check them out as soon as the snow melts," Ricky explained. "I hope to get one of them to take me on as an apprentice so I can really learn about the material."

Rocks, Stephanie thought. I'm sitting here talking about rocks? Come on, girl, you can do better than this. Her eyes began to roam as the band started up another song.

"Must be a relief not to worry about guys anymore," Liz murmured into her ear, "now that you and Jonathan are married."

Stephanie looked at Liz blankly and bit her lip to keep from saying something she would regret. Then, somewhere deep in her chest, she felt a dull ache, a guilty ache.

She hadn't once thought about Jonathan since he'd left, except when someone else brought him up. And she didn't miss him at all.

Michael Gianelli punched the rewind button on the studio's editing machine and stared at the backward motion on the monitor.

The flickering image of the Money Plane meeting came to life for the umpteenth time. There was a medium shot of Jean-Marc and his charts, a pan of the eager crowd, then a pause as the spy cam picked up Nancy in the back of the room.

Michael bristled. He punched the pause button

and stared at Nancy's face, frozen on the screen. "Nancy, you redefine the word *difficult*," he muttered to himself.

He abruptly shut off the machine, grabbed his jacket, and headed out the door. The whirling snowflakes and icy air felt cool against his flushed face. He tromped through the snow, now two inches deeper, trying to shake his thoughts of Nancy.

Everywhere he went, she was there. Every idea he had, she had it, too. Every time he thought he had intimidated her enough to quit the show, she stood firm. She was a wall. A very smart, beautiful wall.

"You're driving me crazy, Nancy Drew," he whispered to himself, balling his hands up into fists. Clusters of students passed him, their frosty breaths mingling in the air.

"Yo—Gianelli!" he heard someone call.

Michael saw a friend hurrying toward him in the semidarkness. "Hey, Brad, my man."

"You're heading over to the Tau Omegas, aren't you?" Brad asked.

"Nope," Michael said. "Going nowhere but home."

"Come on, man," Brad said. "I can't believe you'd pass on this. Everyone's going to be there."

Michael shrugged and followed Brad. The Tau Omegas were famous for their do-or-die parties, exactly the kind of distraction Michael needed.

When they arrived, they felt the warmth from a fire roaring in the fireplace, and even more heat radiating out from the dance floor. Grabbing a drink from a tub of ice, Michael shouldered his way through the crowd. He high-fived his buddies along the way. He loosened up but still felt on shaky ground. What was he going to do with Nancy Drew?

He sat down in a chair by the window and gave himself strict instructions to put her out of his mind and have fun.

"Having fun?" A soprano voice momentarily pulled him away from his thoughts. It was the girl with straw-colored hair from his journalism workshop.

Michael blinked. "Oh, hi. You're—Sandi, right?"

The girl smiled, leaning against the window seat next to his chair. "Right. How's your new show going? I watched the first one. It was great."

"Thanks," Michael said, turning away. There wasn't a terribly strong resemblance between Nancy and Sandi. So why did Nancy's face keep popping up in his mind?

"What are you going to do for your next show?" Sandi asked.

Michael glanced at Sandi, then cleared his throat. Sandi definitely had blue eyes, but they weren't as striking as Nancy's.

"Hel-lo? Earth to Michael. Come in, Michael."

Sandi's hair was blond and very pretty. But it didn't have Nancy's red highlights that caught the light and . . .

Sandi playfully punched him in the arm.

"What?" Michael asked.

"I think you're working too hard," Sandi said, shaking her head as the music started up again. "You aren't listening to a word I say."

"I'm sorry," Michael apologized. "Want to dance?"

She smiled and Michael stood up. He slipped an arm around her waist and led her to the dance floor. She was a good dancer, great even, but he was glad when the music ended and they sat down on a couch near the fireplace.

"So, what's it like being on television?" Sandi asked.

Michael groaned inwardly. He hated those questions. But Sandi's quickly got worse.

"Are you dating your co-host? The girl with the reddish—" Sandi began.

"Nancy Drew? No way. What makes you ask that?" The words came out more forcefully than he wanted.

"Whoa." Sandi laughed. "Touchy subject?"

"It's just that I'm not," Michael said. "We're not. Dating. We just work together.

"In fact, we're working on a story right now," he said lamely, hunting for an excuse to change the subject. "We're doing a story about one of those so-called investment games."

"Oh, not the Money Plane!" Sandi blurted out. "What a rip-off."

Suddenly Michael was interested in what Sandi had to say. "What do you mean?"

Sandi shrugged. "It's a rip-off," she repeated. "I have a friend at Brockton College who paid a hundred and fifty bucks to some guy with a fake name and she never saw her money again."

"Really? What was the guy's name?"

Sandi's eyes twinkled at him. "Ace. Isn't that the dumbest?"

Michael froze. Ace. The redheaded guy with the baseball cap who was at Jean-Marc's meeting.

"Sandi?" Michael asked, just as the music grew louder. He raised his voice. "Can you put me in touch with your friend at Brockton?"

"No problem," Sandi shouted back, slipping a hand in his. She gave him a quick kiss on the cheek. "But give yourself a break and don't work so hard, Michael. Let's dance."

Nancy collapsed into her desk chair. It was ten-thirty, Friday night. She and Kara had dropped in on a wild party, but Nancy had come back early to catch up on some reading. The phone rang almost as soon as Nancy had her nightshirt on.

"Hello?" Nancy said wearily.

"What's the matter with you?" Bess asked without even saying hello.

"Hi, Bess. I'm sorry I didn't stop by your table at the union," Nancy said. "I was angry with Michael."

"Oh, sure," Bess said. "He's really gotten under your skin."

"I know he has," Nancy said. "He's driving me insane with his attitude and his ego and—"

"His tall, dark, and handsome looks," Bess said. "I know he'd drive me crazy. It's no wonder you can't tear yourself away from him to say hello to your oldest and dearest friend."

"Oh, stop," Nancy snapped. She wrapped the telephone cord around her wrist, annoyed. "We needed information from Jean-Marc."

"Was it about that Money Plane game?" Bess asked. "Holly was telling me about it right before you and Michael made your entrance."

"Don't remind me," Nancy said with a groan. "What did Holly have to say about the game?"

"She was sure that Jean-Marc wouldn't intentionally rip people off," Bess answered. "She got offended that I'd even question his integrity."

Nancy felt her face grow hot. "Well, what he's doing is most likely illegal. And, I think a lot of students will wind up losing money."

"Holly says it's completely straight," Bess countered.

"Holly might not know the whole story," Nancy gently asserted, trying not to upset her friend. "Probably all she knows is that Jean-Marc hasn't lost any money himself."

Bess hesitated on the other end of the line before speaking. "Actually, Holly said Jean-Marc didn't have to put up any money."

Nancy froze. "He didn't?"

"No," Bess said slowly. "I think it was because he agreed to recruit—"

"I can't talk," Nancy said suddenly, staring at a figure that had silently appeared in the doorway of her room. For a moment she almost didn't recognize the familiar face. He remained so still, with an expression she'd never seen. For a moment she decided it wasn't Michael after all.

"I'll call you back later, Bess," Nancy murmured.

"Take your time, Nan," Bess said as Nancy hung up.

"Hi," Michael said.

"Ever hear of knocking?" Nancy replied, aware that she had on nothing but a skimpy nightshirt. She quickly threw on her bathrobe.

"Okay, forget it," Michael said, and walked out the door.

"What's up?" Nancy persisted, calling to him from her room. "You came all the way over here. . . ." She hurried out of the suite to follow him into the hall.

Michael stood with his hands in his pockets, waiting for the elevator. Nancy wanted to explode, but Bess's words about his effect on her stopped her.

She tried to look at him objectively. He *was* good-looking, smart, creative, driven. A moment earlier he had been standing at her door, looking very friendly and even slightly appealing. He couldn't be that bad, could he?

Then, a second later, Nancy noticed the bright red smear of lipstick on the side of his face. Something clenched inside her stomach, and she felt all of her doubts flooding back.

"Come on, what is it?" Nancy asked sharply, crossing her arms.

"We've got to get over to Brockton," Michael said. "Tomorrow."

"Why?"

"I got a tip," Michael explained. "A student there knows all about the Money Plane."

Nancy uncrossed her arms, and they fell to her sides. "You're actually telling me about a tip? You're telling me where you're going and asking me to come along?"

Michael's face hardened, and his hands dug deeper into his pockets. "Come if you want. Sidney Trenton would go ballistic if I didn't hold your hand through this one."

"Oh, stow it, big shot," Nancy said. "Just give me the details."

"I met someone who's making arrangements right now to have us get together with this student—a woman who was scammed—tomorrow. I've got directions to her dorm."

Nancy's heart sped up.

"Are you in?" Michael turned to face Nancy. "I'm leaving at eight o'clock tomorrow morning."

Nancy smiled at him. "I'll be ready."

George opened her eyes and stretched. It was early Saturday morning and Jamison Hall was silent. She glanced over at her roommate, Pam Miller, who was snuggled under a down comforter, still asleep.

Shivering, George tiptoed over to the window

and saw that the campus had a fresh pelt of thick snow from the night before. The snow had stopped, but a brisk wind was sending showers of powder cascading down from the trees. Not a single footprint disturbed the plain of snow stretching from her dorm across the campus lawn.

Just then her phone rang. George answered as quickly as she could, but Pam's head had already popped up from her pillow.

"Are you packed?" she heard Will's voice ask her.

"Yeah. Pick me up. It's so beautiful out. I can't wait to get going."

"Hold on, snow queen. Andy's car isn't fixed," Will told her. "They promised it in an hour. Then we'll pick you up and head out."

George sighed, staring at her duffel. "Bummer," she said. "Okay. Meet you in the parking lot in an hour."

She slowly crossed back to the window and stared longingly at the drifts of snow. Above, the sky was steel gray, shedding slight filings of snow.

George's eyes traveled to the corner of her room, where her cross-country skis leaned against the wall. She checked her watch. Then, a second later, she was pulling on her snow bibs and cross-country ski boots.

As soon as she opened the door to Jamison Hall, she felt a blast of invigorating cold air on her face. She ran outside, clamped on her skis, slipped her ski pole straps around her wrists, and pushed off, her long legs gliding confidently across the lawn.

She had just enough time to take the trail around the campus lake before Will and the others picked her up. The snow was so dry that her skis were practically floating.

She kicked ahead faster, trying to shake the annoyance she felt about Andy's car. With this extra delay they'd almost have to turn right around again when they got to Wisconsin.

At least the cross-country skiing couldn't be better, George thought with rising excitement. So much snow had fallen the night before that even the piles of dirty, plowed snow had been transformed into crystal hills. She skirted them, then crossed a main bike path, cutting through the woods to the edge of the lake, where a two-mile long path circled it.

When she reached the frozen lake, a flock of winter birds flew into the air and angled away from her path. There was a No Skating or Skiing on Lake sign along the path, which had been put up earlier in the year after someone fell through the ice and was nearly frozen before being rescued. George shook her head when she saw the tracks of an early morning skier who had ignored the sign.

She pushed ahead along the path, past the row of memorial benches, the outdoor amphitheater, and the snow-laden groundskeeper's shed. The lake was one of George's favorite places. It never failed to refresh her.

As George rounded a bend, the morning stillness was suddenly shaken by a fresh, strong wind from the north. The snow-laden treetops swayed, casting down their heavy loads, and the light ground cover of snow began to kick up into blinding sheets. George felt the temperature drop, and she bent her head against the wind.

She was only a quarter of the way around the lake path when the snow let up and the sky opened briefly to the west. She knew storms like these could sweep in and out quicker than she could snap her fingers. But the prospect of continuing around the lake was too tempting for her to turn back.

She checked her watch. If she kept up her current pace, she'd easily make it around the lake and back to the parking lot in time to meet Will and the others.

She took deep breaths and glided forward in the sudden quiet, aiming for the quaint boat-house that stood about a half-mile ahead on the lake's far shore.

Soozie Beckerman carried a tray of steaming mugs into the Kappas' cozy living room. A fire was crackling in the fireplace, and heavy snow pattered against the windows.

Bess, Holly, and Jean-Marc were fooling around on the Kappa's baby grand piano, doing a punky rendition of "Walking in a Winter Wonderland."

"Our planning meeting for the winter formal

begins in two minutes," Soozie announced, setting the tray down and smoothing her silky hair.

Holly pointed out the window at the swirling snow. "Unless our dorm dwellers are snowed in this morning."

Jean-Marc stood up. "See you guys later. I've got some new snowshoes I want to try out"—he winked at Holly—"*before* I chain myself to my computer and finish my Russian history paper."

"Be careful, Jean-Marc," Bess said as she and Holly followed him to the door. "You can barely see out there."

Jean-Marc was about to open the door when it suddenly flew open and several snowpeople stumbled inside.

"Get me to that fireplace!" Bess heard Casey Fontaine's voice beneath her snow-stiff muffler. "I'm frozen."

"My toes have frostbite," Eileen said between breaths. She sat down and held up her leg for someone to pull off her boot.

"Is it really that bad out there?" Jean-Marc asked with a twinge of disappointment in his voice. "Maybe I'll finish my term paper *before* I go snowshoeing."

Eileen looked up in surprise. "Jean-Marc! You're just the person I need to talk to."

Another troop of snowy creatures crowded through the door in time to hear Eileen.

"Jean-Marc?" a vaguely desperate voice called out. "Where is he? I need to talk to him, too."

Others joined in with a dissonant chorus of "Me, too!" and "Jean-Marc" and "Where is he?"

Bess didn't like the sound of this. How could she and Holly get Jean-Marc out of there?

Jean-Marc put up his hands and started to step back as the group descended on him.

"Whoa!" he tried to joke. "I'm being stampeded."

"Come on." Eileen linked elbows with Jean-Marc and marched him back inside. "You got me into the Money Plane, now you have to give me some advice."

"Yeah," another Kappa spoke up. "There's another meeting tomorrow night, and where are we supposed to find new passengers by then?"

Eileen let go of Jean-Marc in front of the fire and brushed the snow off her sleeves. "Actually, I'm not panicking. A lot of people I've talked to are really interested in buying passenger seats."

The muscles in Jean-Marc's face relaxed. He stuffed his hands in his jean pockets and grinned. "That's right, Eileen. People are flocking to these meetings. You saw that for yourself yesterday."

Another Kappa moved forward. "But a lot of the people I've talked to have already signed onto a pyramid."

Jean-Marc attempted to reassure her. "Look, you just signed on yesterday. It takes a week or two to gather the people you need. But the pay-off is going to make it all worthwhile—isn't it?"

Bess could feel the tension ease as some of the girls trailed off toward the dining room. But there was an uneasy expression on Jean-Marc's face as he said goodbye to Holly. He seemed to be even more in a hurry to get out the door.

"I hope he's right," Eileen confided to Bess after Jean-Marc left. "I had to borrow my money in the first place."

Bess winced.

"But," Eileen said, "assuming I get my twelve hundred dollars in the next few weeks, I can pay it back and have money for my sorority dues, plus the expenses my parents decided are *my* responsibility now."

"It'll work out," Bess reassured her.

"Well, Jean-Marc said it was a sure thing," Eileen said. "And he's Holly's boyfriend."

Bess was glad she hadn't invested any money and wondered if Nancy had discovered anything new that morning. Bess thought Eileen *should* be worried.

CHAPTER 4

Let's go over my interview questions before we get to Brockton College," Nancy said, flipping open her notebook and settling into the passenger seat of Michael's red VW beetle.

Minutes earlier Nancy had met Michael in the Thayer Hall parking lot. More snow had fallen the night before, but the roads had been plowed and they made it easily through downtown Weston to the highway.

"Aha, now it's *your* interview?" Michael asked with a sarcastic laugh. "I'm so sorry, Lois Lane."

Nancy dropped her notebook. "You want to ask the questions on camera? Fine."

"No, go ahead," Michael insisted. "It hasn't seemed to hurt us to have your pretty face on camera. After all, I can't do *everything.*"

"Really?" Nancy said. "If I'm Lois Lane, I thought that would make you Superman."

"I didn't want to say anything, but there is a

strong resemblance, isn't there?" Michael flashed Nancy a dazzling smile.

Nancy had to resist smiling back.

"Let's settle on the questions beforehand. I don't want you to spring anything on this woman that doesn't relate to what we're after," Michael said.

Nancy bit her tongue to control her frustration. "What else would I ask her about? I'm not into talk-show gossip. I just want to do a straight interview, step-by-step: What happened? Who does she think ripped her off? How much did she lose? Basic journalism. Then I want to get into her feelings a little. We *should* touch on the emotional side to this story. I imagine she feels pretty stupid, getting taken like that."

"Okay, fine," Michael said quietly, which Nancy took as a possible truce. Being with Michael was like riding an emotional roller coaster. He went from being infuriating to charming in a matter of seconds. Nancy never knew what to expect or how to feel.

She shook the roller-coaster image from her head and looked out at the passing scenery. Eight-foot-high snowdrifts had been left on each side of the road by the snowplows. Clean, sparkling, untouched snow lay under a blue sky, but dark clouds gathered to the north.

For most of the time, the co-hosts rode in silence, with only the occasional comment on the weather. Nancy sensed that Michael was trying harder to get along, if only for the sake of the show.

"There's the Brockton exit," Nancy said, pointing to the right.

"Great, now we're in business." Michael picked up a slip of paper with the directions from the dashboard.

He found a parking spot right outside Diane Schmidt's dorm. "Ten o'clock. Right on time."

"Nice driving," Nancy muttered. All of this pleasant chatter was starting to get on her nerves.

"I felt so stupid," Diane Schmidt was saying as Nancy and Michael set up her dorm room for the interview. "I spent money that was supposed to go for my books on that rip-off pyramid scheme."

"Just a minute," Michael said, clipping a mike to her collar. He stepped back, checked the battery on the video camera, then tightened the screws on the tripod.

Nancy glanced over at Michael, who gave her the thumbs-up sign. "Okay, Diane."

"That's why I couldn't believe it when my friend Sandi called and said you guys were doing a story on the same scam at Wilder," Diane explained. "I'm really glad you contacted me."

"Do you know how many others lost money?" Nancy asked her.

"Dozens got burned," Diane said, her eyes flashing. She raked her frizzy red hair back with her fingers and glanced toward the door. "Some of them are good friends of mine. They'd love for this thing to get out. I asked some of them to stop by. Maybe they could help you out, too."

Nancy and Michael exchanged satisfied looks. They had endured a two-hour drive over snowy roads that morning, but it was going to pay off big-time for *Headlines*.

"Tell us how the game started at Brockton," Nancy asked her.

"Last spring I met this guy at a dorm party," Diane explained. "He seemed nice enough, and we got to talking about this investment game he called the Money Plane."

Nancy nodded.

Diane took a breath. "He told me how he'd paid one hundred fifty dollars, and in less than two weeks he got back twelve hundred dollars— enough money for a down payment on a Jeep."

There was a knock at the door. "Hey, Diane," a girl's voice called. "We're here to talk to the people from Wilder."

Nancy signaled for Michael to keep the camera rolling. Diane walked to the door and opened it to a group of six or seven students, who trooped angrily into the room.

"This is Nancy Drew and Michael Gianelli from Wilder," Diane explained. "They've been investigating the Money Plane scam. They're trying to find out who's behind it."

Nancy cleared her throat. "You guys are welcome to stay, and we'd like to get your comments on camera, too."

The group murmured their agreement and then hushed to listen to Diane's story.

"Anyway," Diane went on, "I stupidly paid him the money, hoping I could get my twelve hundred dollars in time for my next tuition payment. But I bought in too late. Ace's explanation was that there just weren't enough new players to push me into the pilot's seat. Finally I had to tell my parents I'd blown the money. They were furious."

Nancy's eyes widened. "The guy's name was Ace?"

Michael looked up from the camera. "Tall, with red hair and a baseball cap?"

"That's him." Diane nodded. "That's what he called himself, anyway. It wasn't his real name."

"Their use of code names will make them just that much more difficult to track down," Nancy said.

"So the same guy is ripping people off at Wilder?" Diane asked, shaking her head.

Nancy nodded. "It's got to be the same guy. Your description matches that of the Ace who's pushing the game at Wilder."

"Yeah, but Ace isn't the only one," a guy in a ski cap spoke up. "My contact's name was Bullet. Same deal. I paid the one hundred fifty bucks because I needed spending money for my semester in Rome." He rubbed his face, and Michael got an excellent head shot that showed all his embarrassment and anger at being swindled. "Not only did I feel like an idiot when it didn't pay out, I couldn't even afford to pay for my semester abroad anymore."

One of the girls squared her shoulders. "Our contact called himself Fly. By the time we got into the game, there wasn't anyone left to recruit."

"Money Plague is more like it," Dianne interjected. Her friends nodded in agreement, but no one found it funny.

"Okay, let's stop for a moment," Michael said hurriedly. "This is turning into a bigger interview than we planned. I've got to put a fresh tape into the camera."

Nancy squeezed onto the bed between students and took notes.

Nancy felt a mixture of sympathy and bewilderment as she did her interviews. After all, she thought, didn't anyone take math? The simple arithmetic told the story better than anything. A pyramid had to split three times before a "passenger" could collect twelve hundred dollars. And eight new passengers had to be recruited each time to split. That meant that twenty-four students had to pay one hundred fifty dollars for one to get twelve hundred dollars.

There would always be too many planes and not enough passengers. It didn't take a whole lot of brain power to figure that out, but Nancy knew that cash-strapped college students were easy prey for money-making schemes. Meanwhile, Ace—or Jean-Marc—took away one hundred fifty dollars for every student who didn't "fly away."

"What was I supposed to do?" Diane said when Michael turned the camera back on. She looked sheepish. "Call the police? I didn't even know the guy's name. I felt totally embarrassed that I'd been scammed."

"We knew it was against school regulations when we paid," one of the girls added, "but we didn't know it was against the law. We found out later, and that's when we decided to lay low."

"Does anyone know Ace's real name?" Nancy wanted to know.

"Never found out," Diane said. "In fact, I hardly saw him after I paid in my money. I figure he just stuck all the cash in a suitcase and moved on."

Michael put the camera on pause. "Okay, folks. I need to confer with Nancy for a minute. I'll leave the camera rolling and you just say what you want while we step outside." He started the tape rolling and motioned Nancy into the hallway.

"Good idea, Michael, just letting them talk. We might get some really good footage," Nancy said, sincerely impressed.

"Or we might get garbage" was Michael's response.

Nancy shrugged. "Do you think Jean-Marc knows Ace's real name?" she asked.

"You bet he does," Michael insisted. "They were collecting money side by side at the Thayer Hall meeting."

Nancy shook her head. "That doesn't prove anything."

"It sure says a lot," Michael argued.

"I *know*," Nancy said. "He's certainly guilty of something, but I just can't see Jean-Marc knowingly ripping off his friends."

Michael shrugged. "You have a high opinion of your friend's intellect. Is this Jean-Marc really that *stupid?* The way I see it, he got greedy and feels he has nothing to lose."

"Except his friends," Nancy reminded him.

"Come on, Nancy. Don't be so naive. Not everyone has their priorities as straight as you do."

Nancy frowned. That was an underhanded compliment if she'd ever heard one. "Let's get the whole story," she said, "before we condemn him."

Nancy checked her watch, then looked out the hallway window and groaned. The snow was falling harder than ever. "We'd better get on the road if we want to make it back to Wilder."

Michael joined Nancy at the window. "Whew," he said, "it looks wicked out there." They went back into Diane's room and waited while the guy in the ski cap finished what he was saying.

"Thanks, everyone," Michael said when the guy was done. "With what we've got, we should be able to blow this guy's airplane scam wide open."

"Thank *you*. It'll be sweet revenge if you can get those jerks," Diane responded. "Do you think maybe you should stick around until the highway is plowed again? I'd be glad to show you around campus."

"Thanks, but we're going to have to get to work on this tape as soon as possible if we're going to make our deadline."

"And give those bums the exposure they deserve," said one of Diane's friends.

Nancy suddenly had a vision of Jean-Marc's face in the union after the Thayer Hall meeting. He had looked exhausted, but what did that mean? Was he nervous about the possible grounding of the Money Plane? Or maybe he wasn't so sure himself that he was selling a fool-proof investment?

"Okay," Michael said after they'd packed their gear. "We're ready to hit the road. Thanks again."

Nancy had her hand on the doorknob when Diane spoke once more.

"Wait, there's one more thing."

"What's that?" Nancy asked.

"I didn't say anything earlier because I couldn't quite remember," Diane said. "But now I have. Goldfinger."

"As in the James bond movie *Goldfinger?*" Michael asked rather snidely.

"No," Diane continued and turned away from Michael to talk to Nancy. "It was something Ace said. He said he'd learned a thing or two from a guy named Goldfinger—the guy who'd taught him all about the business."

"A guy? Who taught him?" Nancy asked.

"Yeah," Diane said. "But I guess it could be a woman. He said Goldfinger taught him everything he needed to know about money."

"Ooof," George uttered wearily. She stopped and braced herself against her ski poles. The whirling snow had thickened and the wind was pushing hard against her chest even as she stood still.

She'd been enjoying the snowfall and the view of the wooden boathouse just ahead on the trail. But then a fierce wind had roared in, and the picturesque panorama suddenly became a terrifyingly white blank.

George tucked her head into the wind and pushed on a few yards, but the snow was like sharp bits of sand, scouring every bit of her exposed skin. She stopped again to get a glimpse of the boathouse up ahead. Now it was nowhere to be seen. All around her boiled a cold, trackless sea of white. Lake blended into trail and trail into woods.

Suddenly her bearings were gone. She no longer knew where she was or which direction she was supposed to be going.

The cold pressed in, making her feel claustrophobic, and the snow was piling up so thick around her ankles she could barely move forward. "Stay calm, George." She spoke to herself reassuringly, balling her fingers up inside her gloves for momentary warmth. "Just keep moving. You're bound to run into something."

With the shriek of the wind in her ears, George pushed on steadily for what seemed forever.

Inevitably she had to slow. Her head pounded with the cold, and she felt her eyelids droop from exhaustion. It would be tempting to curl up in a ball and take a brief rest, George thought groggily. Sleep might just be the best thing. . . .

"Ouch!" George cried out as the tip of one of her skis jammed into something hard, jarring her knee. With great effort she leaned forward and felt a hard surface. A boulder? A wall? The boathouse.

Inching forward on her skis, she felt along its perimeter until her gloves grazed a latch. She fumbled with it, her hands nearly frozen. She knew there had to be a door attached to the latch, but try as hard as she could, she couldn't figure out how to open it. Icy tears started to travel down her cheeks.

George couldn't stop the exasperated sob that slipped out of her. She would not and could not be defeated by a blizzard, she told herself. With one great burst of angry strength, she slammed her body against the door and moved it into the boathouse by sheer force of will.

She slammed the door shut behind her and stumbled in the sudden quiet and darkness of the boathouse.

"Are you all right?" The voice seemed to come from far away.

"Let me sleep," George mumbled sleepily, slipping to the floor and curling onto her side.

She felt someone release her ski bindings and lift her into a sitting position. The someone then pulled off her frozen gloves, and she felt warm hands on hers. Slowly, a man's face began to take shape before her in the dim light.

"Here," he said, brushing snow off her jacket. "Let me help you with those goggles."

George felt her goggles being peeled off, and then found herself staring into a pair of clear, blue eyes.

"I'm Ross Yaeger," the man said. "Are you okay? How long have you been out there?"

"I think I'm okay," George said. "But now that I'm halfway conscious, I think I was in pretty bad shape." She studied Ross Yaeger for a moment. His curly brown hair was flattened, and his polar fleece running gear was damp. In the dim light, she could see that he was probably in his late twenties. He had a taut, athlete's body and a squarish face that looked determined but kind.

"I'm crazy enough to be out here, too," Ross said, his eyes twinkling at her. "Only I was on snowshoes."

"Ross Yaeger," George said softly to herself. "Your name is familiar."

"I'm on the faculty," he responded. "English department. Romantic period. Nineteenth century."

George stared. Montana Smith's campus radio call-in program had voted Ross Yaeger the hottest professor at Wilder. Every woman who'd ever taken his class had a crush on him. His smile left no question why.

"I have only one of these," he said, pulling out a shiny space blanket from his pack and opening it up. "So we'd better share it. It looks like we're going to be here for a while."

"My fingers are too cold to work on this riff," Ray Johansson said, setting down his guitar and slipping his hands under his armpits.

Cory McDermott looked up from his bass guitar and shook his head. "At least I've still got power to run this baby," he said, patting his guitar.

"For now," Ray pointed out.

"If the power goes out on our electric space heaters, we'll need this stove more than ever," Montana Smith said, poking a stick in the loft's ancient wood-burning stove. She shut its little door and held her slender fingers out for warmth. "Austin says there's plenty of wood stacked in the cellar. He's coming back with some."

"Good," Karin Messer said, blowing a large bubble, then snapping it back in her mouth. "It's a meat locker in here." She ran a fast series of minor chords on her electric keyboard before yanking her leather jacket up from the floor and putting it on.

"I hope this storm doesn't wipe out our practice time this weekend," Ray said. "Our next gig is in five days, and I want to be on top of it."

"It'll work out, Ray," Montana said soothingly. "You guys sound better than ever."

Ray nodded. Actually, his new group, Radical Moves, was turning into a big success. They were booked every weekend for the next couple of months. A club in Chicago wanted to audition them. And they finally had enough money to cut a demo to send out to some major music producers.

"Here we go," the band's drummer, Austin Ruche, called out as he backed through the door with an armload of wood.

"Let's go outside and check out the storm," Montana said, "while Austin warms up this place."

Ray watched as Montana sprang up and Cory tenderly pulled a hat over her head of very curly blond hair. Recently, Cory and Montana had started dating, and it had been a relief to Ray. Ever since his breakup with Ginny Yuen, Montana had been coming on to him. At first Ray had enjoyed the attention, but the thrill hadn't lasted. He and Montana were the best of friends, but he knew deep inside he wasn't over Ginny.

"Get a move on, Ray," Montana ordered him from downstairs. She dragged Cory out through the front door and into the snow.

Ray shrugged and pulled on his jacket. Outside, the snow was falling so hard they could barely see the trees surrounding the building. Drifts of snow were piling up, and it looked as if another six inches of snow had fallen on their cars in the last hour.

"Watch this!" Montana shouted. She fell backward into the snow. Cory and Ray laughed as Montana waved her arms and legs in the snow, then carefully stood up and pointed. "An angel."

Cory whooped and lumbered through the snow toward her. His ruddy face was glowing and wisps of his red hair blew in the wind. "You *are* an angel."

Ray felt a clutch in his chest as Cory grabbed Montana with his brawny arms. They kissed, then fell sideways into the soft snow. He reminded himself that he was relieved Montana had gotten together with Cory.

It was crazy. Maybe it was the weather. Maybe it was the music. But he was starting to see Montana differently. He stared at her, frolicking in the snow, her blond hair flying. She was beautiful and smart. She *had* pursued him, and now . . . He thought hard, trying to remember why he had let her slip away.

"There's a gas station," Nancy cried. "Let's pull over."

"You're seeing things." Michael squinted through the windshield as the wipers pumped furiously.

Nancy braced herself as Michael's little VW skidded back and forth in the ruts of snow. "This is a blizzard, Michael," she shouted. "You can't see the highway any more than I can. We'll never make it back at this rate."

Michael gripped the steering wheel and wiped

the inside of the windshield at the same time. "Piece of cake. I've driven in worse weather."

"You're either crazy or stupid," Nancy said, holding her head.

"The craziest thing I could do would be to risk getting snowbound with you." Michael turned to Nancy and smiled wickedly.

This time Nancy couldn't help herself, and she threw her head back, laughing. His smile was just so contagious.

Then, suddenly, the car fishtailed and the snow enveloped them in a whiteout. Michael started pumping the brakes furiously.

"Careful, there might be someone behind us," Nancy warned.

Michael let out an exasperated breath and rolled down his window, trying to get his bearings. A gust of icy flakes blew in.

"The gas station was just a few hundred yards back," Nancy said. "Let's wait it out in there."

Michael nodded grimly and stepped lightly on the accelerator. "I think there's a place up ahead where I can turn around . . . I think I can just make it out—"

"Look out!" Nancy cried.

Michael turned the wheel abruptly as the highway suddenly twisted around a bend. The car headed into a spin like some kind of carnival ride.

Nancy wrapped her arms around her head just as the car dipped down in front and plunged off the road.

"Hold on!" Michael shouted. The car crashed through several small trees and nearly turned over before ramming ferociously into something hard.

Nancy felt her elbow strike the windshield as they slammed to a stop. She fell back into the seat, stunned.

Nancy didn't know if it had been a minute or an hour that she had been sitting, staring at the cracked windshield before her. She looked at Michael and saw that he had hit his head against the steering wheel. Nancy felt her stomach lurch as he slumped to one side, a trail of blood trickling down from the gash in his forehead.

CHAPTER 5

Nancy struggled frantically to pry herself out of the front passenger-side corner of the smashed VW bug. She began to panic. Snow and wind were blowing in through the broken windshield. She couldn't get out.

Then she took a deep breath. Don't think, she told herself. Relax. Breathe. Her mind slowly began to refocus, and she managed to pull her legs out from between the creases of metal that had collapsed around them.

The VW was now firmly wedged against a tree.

Michael groaned, lifted his head, and opened his eyes wide with concern and alarm. "Nancy, are you hurt?"

"Just my elbow," she answered softly, gripping her arm. "But I think it's just banged up. Nothing serious. But you, Michael, are you hurt?"

"I'm okay," Michael whispered. He reached

out and caught her hand and gripped it tightly. Nancy stared into his deep brown eyes.

Michael reached over and brushed her hair away from her forehead. "If anything—" he began as Nancy said, "You're bleeding, Michael. You've hit your head. Do you have a first-aid kit?"

Michael shook his head and groaned. "No, no first-aid kit. We need to get out of here," he said, working his door open.

Nancy felt her face flush, with anger or relief, she wasn't sure. "You don't stop your car during blizzards. You don't carry a first-aid kit. And you never ask for directions. You must really think you *are* Superman," she said.

"We wouldn't be here if you hadn't startled me when I was driving." Michael yanked the camera pack out from the back and slipped it over one shoulder.

"Oh, so now this is my fault?" Nancy cried, following him out of the driver's side door. She had difficulty finding her footing in the deep snow of the steep ravine.

"You shouted, I instinctively put on the brakes and spun out," Michael argued as they began climbing to the top of the ravine.

"Are you kidding? If I hadn't seen that curve, you would have taken us off the road at thirty miles an hour instead of five. Obviously, that head injury hasn't improved your mind or personality."

"I'm sorry." Michael reached up and held his head. "I'm not mad at you. It's not your fault.

Let's just head back toward the gas station you saw. We passed a farmhouse, too, and it was even closer."

Nancy made it to the top of the slope and stepped out on the road. The blowing snow nearly blinded her. "Michael, wait," she shouted, shielding her face from the stinging flakes. "We can't go anywhere in these conditions. Especially you. You have a head injury. Maybe we should wait in the car until the storm passes."

"No way," Michael shouted, climbing onto the shoulder of the highway. "We have no food or heat—and who knows how long it will be until the storm passes. Come on, or we'll freeze to death."

As they walked into the blinding snow, Nancy zipped her jacket to the very top. Her instinct was to stay put in the car, but she couldn't let Michael wander off by himself. He was still bleeding. He might even have a concussion.

For reasons she couldn't explain, her feelings for Michael right then were overwhelming. Just as he almost disappeared ahead of her into the snow, she staggered after him.

"I love a good blackout," Stephanie cracked, sauntering around the pool table in the first-floor lounge at Thayer Hall. Candles were set up all around the room, sending out flickering yellow light. "Candlelight is sexy."

Ginny steadied her cue and shot the number seven ball crisply into a side pocket. She stood up, dug her hands into her jacket pockets, and smiled. "I'm finally beginning to appreciate your attitude, Steph. I almost wish you hadn't moved out on us to get married."

Two hours earlier a huge branch from one of the oldest trees on campus had snapped and fallen across a power line. Most of the older university buildings were in the dark, but modern Thayer Hall wasn't completely blacked out. It had a backup generator that kept the heat and a few dim lights working.

Everywhere, parties had popped up spontaneously. Food stashes were dug out and shared. Bowling games had sprouted in the halls using wastecans as pins and various round objects for balls. Outside, the howling snowstorm refused to let up.

"At least the vending machines are working," Dawn Steiger, Ginny's resident advisor, said as Ginny lined up her shot.

Stephanie shook her head. "You're out of luck, Dawn. The machines may be working, but when I walked by, they were empty. Even the chocolate-covered marshmallow treats were gone."

Ginny hit the cue ball with a little too much force, and the five ball bounced off the bumpers of a corner pocket. "The Thayer cafeteria is closed," she said, "but maybe the main cafeteria is open."

"The snow's too deep for the kitchen staff to get in," Stephanie said, easily sinking the two ball. "I bet it isn't open, either."

"I sure hope we can find something to eat that isn't junk food," Ginny said wistfully, her stomach grumbling. "It's a medical fact that college students—especially pre-med students—can't survive more than ten hours without food."

Male laughter rose from the doorway. "Don't believe a word of it," a voice rode on top of the noise.

Ginny turned and grinned. It was Ricky Perelis, the guy Liz had introduced her to the night before at the Cave.

"Ricky! What are you doing here?" she asked.

"We—that's Scott, Blake, Donald, Rusty, and I"—Ricky pointed out each of his friends, who took a bow when introduced—"we thought we'd check out the action in all the dorms on campus."

"We just put on our warmest clothes and slogged our way through," Scott interjected.

"And we thought," Ricky continued, "that we'd save the best for last. And here you are."

"You guys have the pioneer spirit," Stephanie called. "You'll trudge through snow and ice for a party. Hi, I'm Stephanie."

Ricky's friends headed out to scout out the upper floors, while Ricky stayed behind. "Catch you later," he called after them. "You know where I am if nothing's cooking anywhere else."

Ginny leaned over the table to eyeball her next shot.

Ricky's deep-set eyes were smiling as he stood back and watched her just miss sinking the three ball into the side pocket with a bank shot. "You were robbed," he said chivalrously.

"She doesn't have a chance," Stephanie murmured as she walked by him.

Ginny smiled as Stephanie shifted into gear. Watching Stephanie flirt was like observing an artist at work: intense, creative, and completely determined. Taking a cube of blue chalk from the corner of the pool table, Stephanie worked it into the tip of her cue, not once taking her eyes off Ricky. As soon as she thought she had his undivided attention, she refocused on her pool game. She chose the most difficult shot, requiring her to bend way over the table, so the back of her skirt barely covered the tops of her legs.

"How are you coping, Ginny?" Ricky asked her.

"Fine, really, except that I'm starving," she admitted. "But at least we have heat. They lost it over at Jamison."

Stephanie sank the twelve ball with a crack. No one noticed.

"Those older buildings don't have a chance," Ricky pointed out, leaning against the pool table. "They were built without much insulation and wired in the early part of the century."

Stephanie walked around the table and gave Ricky a sultry look. "Excuse me," she said. Ricky raised himself off the edge of the table and moved aside. Stephanie set up her shot right where he'd been warming the felt.

"Oh, great," Ginny said in response to Stephanie's ramming the sixteen ball hard into the pocket next to her. "I'm done for. . . ."

"I'm working on a design for an earth-bermed structure," Ricky went on, "that would hold its heat for days during a power outage like this."

"Excuse me again," Stephanie said breathily, and Ricky stepped aside again.

"Stephanie?" Dawn broke in. She waited until she had Stephanie's attention, then glanced meaningfully at Ginny. Dawn obviously wanted to put a stop to Stephanie's antics. "Do you have any change? I'm dying for something from the machine. There's got to be something left in one of them."

Stephanie glared at Dawn, then flounced away in search of her purse. Ginny was a little embarrassed at Dawn's intervention, and she hoped Ricky hadn't noticed. She didn't want him to think that she and her friends were performing matchmaking maneuvers. Still, she liked him. He was cute, and he had a quiet practicality that attracted her.

"Psst, Ginny," Ricky said under his breath, nodding toward the door. "How would you like to go on a secret mission?"

"Well, that depends on what it is," Ginny said with one eyebrow raised.

"Let me rephrase my question. Do you want to get something to eat?" He grinned a mischievous grin.

Ginny laughed. "Of course I do. I'm starved. But how do you propose to dig through an acre of drifting snow in the middle of a blizzard to search for something?"

Ricky's eyes twinkled at her as he took the cue out of her hand. "Watch me."

Bess dropped her head back on the Kappas' living room couch. Then she rolled it back and forth and crossed her eyes. "I'm crazy. I know I'm crazy."

"No, you're not," Casey said cheerfully, scooting next to her. "You're just a party animal."

Bess blew her bangs straight up. "I'm the expert on having fun, am I?"

"Yep," Holly said matter-of-factly.

Bess watched the last of the Kappas retire from the three-hour Winter Formal planning session. So far, Bess had agreed to be on the food committee and the invitations committee, and to chair the music committee.

"Now I have to line up an entire night's worth of fantastic dance music," Bess thought out loud, chewing on her pencil's eraser and staring into space. "What a blast."

Casey nudged her. "Your interest in planning the music doesn't have anything to do with Max Ridgefield, does it?"

"Oh, no," Holly drawled. "I mean, he *is* a professional party DJ, but Bess couldn't have been thinking of *that.*"

Bess gave them all her best "Who, me?" expression. She patted her sweater pocket, where she had Max's tape that still hadn't been played.

It made her a little sad that Max had had to break their date for tonight, but Bess understood. Just thinking about spending more time with Max stirred Bess.

"Come on," Bess said, standing up and grabbing Holly's hand. "I need to play something on your tape deck."

"What's that noise?" Casey wondered as they headed for the staircase. She peeked out the window in the front door and gasped. "Yay! They're plowing the road out front."

Holly joined her. "Not exactly. It looks like we'll be entertaining the snowplow driver, too."

There was a loud knock at the door, and Holly opened it wide.

"Is Bess Marvin here?" a big guy in a fluorescent jacket hollered above the wind.

"Yes, I'm here," Bess called back. "Come in and close the door."

"Max Ridgefield wants me to get you over to that party he's DJing," the guy said, stomping his feet on the already soaked doormat. "It's on my way."

A big smile stretched across Bess's face as Casey and Holly stared enviously. "That Max Ridgefield is completely crazy," she said, grabbing her jacket, hat, and gloves from the front hall closet. "And I love it!"

"I can't see a thing!" Nancy cried out.

"Just keep moving," Michael's muffled voice called. She could see the dim, grainy outline of his arm waving her on. "Follow the sound of my voice."

"For the first time I'm glad you have such a big mouth," Nancy called up to him.

A lock of frozen hair whipped painfully against Nancy's face as she stumbled blindly along the edge of the highway. They'd been walking along the road for about twenty minutes and still hadn't found the gas station or the farmhouse Michael said he had spotted earlier.

Nancy could no longer feel her toes in her boots. Her hands stung. Her ears ached, not to mention the elbow she had banged when the car crashed. The cold pressed in on her.

Michael had stopped and was waiting for her to catch up. "We've got to find shelter pretty soon."

Nancy just nodded. It was all she could do to put one foot in front of the other through the endless, drifting snow. Then, just when she was sure she couldn't move another inch, the dim outline of something solid appeared off to her left.

"Michael!" she cried, pointing toward the shape. Her voice came out hoarse and cracked, as it sounded after a Wilder Vikings football game.

Together, they stumbled off the highway and plunged waist-deep through a field of heavy drifts. Finally they reached what turned out to be a run-down barn. Nancy found the door, but couldn't get it open. When Michael pulled with her, it creaked open.

"We made it," Michael gasped, collapsing on

an ancient bale of hay and pulling off his sodden hat.

Nancy staggered a few steps inside and fell down next to Michael, vowing never to move again. Her eyes filled with tears. She hadn't admitted, even to herself, how frightened she had felt in the relentless storm. But now her defenses were melting away.

She lay on her back next to Michael, numb with relief. Snow swirled in through holes in the barn's roof, but they were safe at last.

But how long would they be trapped together in this barn?

CHAPTER 6

Okay, Ray and Cory both want a double burger with bacon, large fries, and a cola." Montana was reading from a slip of paper. "Karin wants a veggie burger with onion rings, and for Austin, a coffee and a Munchomaniac with everything."

"Check," Ray and Cory said.

Montana gave Cory an affectionate look. Since the power had gone out, Cory and Ray had been jamming on their acoustical guitars around the stove. Candlelight filled the tiny space.

"If the Bumblebee Diner has power, I should be back with dinner in a half-hour," Montana called, grabbing her down jacket and heading out into the wind and snow.

"Hey, Montana," she heard a voice behind her, turned, and saw Ray rushing out the door as he yanked on his jacket. "I'm going with you."

Montana stared as he ran around to the passenger door and slid in next to her.

"You shouldn't be out here by yourself."

Montana's eyes opened wide. Ray smiled. Bits of melting snow glistened in his short, rumpled hair. "It could be dangerous."

Montana smiled back and started the engine while Ray grabbed a scraper and jumped outside to clear her windshield.

"What is this?" Montana muttered to herself, watching Ray through the glass. "You don't have to convince me you're wonderful, Ray. I'm supposed to be over you. Remember?"

"Driver," Ray called out as he jumped back into the front seat. "The Bumblebee Diner, and step on it."

Montana giggled.

Ray switched on the radio. Montana smiled and looked across at him when she heard the song, the one she'd wanted him to perform right after he put the Radical Moves band together.

"Remember this?" Ray asked with a wink.

Montana laughed and backed her car onto the street. She could barely make out where the sidewalk ended and the street began. But somehow it didn't matter. Montana remembered how out-of-control she had felt when she first introduced herself to Ray. It had been right after he lost his Beat Poets band, and she'd introduced him to Cory and Austin. She'd fallen for him instantly, but Ray had just broken up with Ginny Yuen and he'd been as responsive as a rock.

"Power's on downtown." Ray raised a victory

fist as they passed a row of bright storefronts. "We're eating."

Montana's stomach growled. "I can almost taste my burger."

Ray laughed and slipped his arm along the back of the seat. She felt his fingers tickle the back of her neck.

Inside the diner the booths were jammed and the waiting area was packed with customers wanting take-out orders. Still, Montana could see that everyone was taking the wait in stride. A Little Richard tune was blasting from the sound system, and a couple in ski jackets had started dancing in the space next to the cash register.

Ray slipped an arm around her waist and led her into their own dance.

Montana felt a tiny crack forming in her defenses. She stared up at his handsome face. All this time she'd longed for the smallest signal from him. So what was happening now? And what about Cory?

"Look at this," Ray cried as the cashier finally handed them their order in four huge white paper bags. "You couldn't have carried this back by yourself."

"What would I have done without you?" Montana joked, taking two of the bags and backing out the door.

They laughed the entire way back to the loft. About lousy music. About bad radio. About pretentious music professors. But by the time they got back to the loft, Cory, Austin, and Karin had stopped jamming and were waiting impatiently by the stove.

"What took you so long?" Cory asked.

"Nothing." Montana giggled. "Well, actually . . ."

"They made us dance for our dinner," Ray said with a laugh, setting down the bags and pulling the change out of his pocket.

"Glad you had a good time," Cory said.

When Montana looked at him, she could see that his eyes were like two dark, angry stones in the candlelight.

"Where is she?" Will cried, slamming the phone down.

"Still can't get hold of George?" Andy looked up with alarm from his card game with Reva.

"No," Will said. It was early evening, and he hadn't been able to reach George to tell her that they'd canceled the ski trip.

Reva put down her cards and stood up. "Have you been to the student union? The gym?"

Will felt his gut twist. "Yes, yes. I've been everywhere. But the point is, she would have called to let me know where she was if—if she could."

Will pressed his forehead against the frosty windowpane. Outside, the wind continued to twist the snow along the road.

"You left a message on her machine?" Reva asked.

Will spun around. "We've been through this, Reva. I've left twenty messages. I've told her the ski trip was canceled. I've told her to call because we're worried. I've told her and told her . . ."

"Will," Reva said gently, "please, stop."

"Stop? Take a look outside!" Will shouted. "It's getting dark. What if she's lost out there? What if she's hurt?"

"Calm down, Will. I know you're upset. We all are," Reva said, and their eyes locked. "I think it's time to call the police."

" 'The wild winds weep. And the night is a-cold; Come hither, Sleep, and my grief's infold.' "

George closed her eyes. "That was beautiful, Ross."

"Yeah," the professor agreed. He turned on his side, propped his head on his hand, and stared at her. "The Romantic poets loved snowstorms like this one."

George pulled her half of the blanket up around her chin. The pile of sailcloth they'd found in a corner had been molded into a sort of reclining couch for the two of them. "Well, maybe if the Romantic poets had portable propane heaters and flashlights like we just found," she drawled.

"Poor old poets." Ross laughed.

"Lucky us." George smiled. There was something wonderful about Ross's laugh. For the last several hours George had felt as if she were talking to an old friend. She had to keep reminding herself that he was a professor and she was a student.

By now it was pitch-black outside, and the storm continued to shriek. Hours ago they'd tried making a run for civilization, but the blizzard had been too strong, and they'd turned back after only a few minutes. Luckily, the boathouse's supply box had contained a space heater and flashlight. Ross had even found some trail mix in his jacket pocket.

"I know my friends are worried about me," George said with a sigh. "But it's funny. I don't really mind being stranded."

Ross popped a raisin into his mouth. "I'll take adventure over routine any day."

"You bet," George said in total agreement.

"If I had my way," Ross went on, "I'd find a nice piece of land in the mountains, build a cabin, and spend a lot of time hiking, fishing, reading, and writing."

"Yep," George agreed. "It's funny how I feel most like myself when I'm out running or camping in the woods."

"But we have to work for a living, don't we?" Ross said softly. "Get an education . . ."

George looked at Ross, and for a long moment their eyes locked. Strangely, the urge to drop her gaze politely just wasn't there.

"What are you thinking?" Ross asked, nudging her with his shoulder.

"I wish that I could be very, very sure of what I'm doing with my life," George said.

"Me, too," Ross confessed. "But who is—sure, that is?"

George felt warm inside, and the warmth seemed to zip out to her fingers and toes. Ross was smiling at her as if she was the most fascinating, important person he'd ever spoken to. She shuddered.

"You're cold," Ross said, pulling the loose end of a sail around them both.

George rested her neck against his sturdy arm. Somewhere in the back of her mind, she knew that Ross Yaeger was a college professor. But what really mattered right then, George thought, was that she wanted to go on talking with him all night. They had so much more to say to each other.

Nancy was packing hay around her body for warmth.

"What are you doing?"

"Trying to stay warm. I can't stop thinking," Nancy said, "what would have happened if we hadn't found this barn. We'd be frozen to death by now."

"But we did find the barn." Michael was sitting a few feet from her in the soft hay.

Nancy closed her eyes, exhausted. The wind howled through the cracks in the barn walls. Snow continued to filter down through the holes in the ceiling.

"I got you into this mess. . . ." Michael finally said.

Nancy opened one eye. "That's quite an admission."

Michael flopped on his stomach, put his chin on his fist, and stared at her. "It's true that I dug up the story idea. It's true that I found Diane, who just gave us a killer interview for the show. I'm sorry, Nancy. Really I am."

Nancy covered her eyes in frustration. "If you must talk, don't talk about the show. Don't talk about anything that's happened today."

"Mmm. Okay," Michael said after a thoughtful pause. "Let's interview each other. I'll go first," Michael said eagerly, sitting up and grasping his knees. "Where were you born? Did you have a happy childhood?"

Nancy sighed. "I was born in River Heights, Illinois, to Mr. and Mrs. Drew. My father was a lawyer, and my mother took care of me."

"Go on."

"I was happy. We lived in a beautiful home and my father and I were very close. I took horseback riding and ballet and piano lessons. I had chicken pox but recovered. My best friends were—and are—Bess Marvin and her cousin, George Fayne. I went out with a really good guy named Ned Nickerson."

"Whoa," Michael broke in. "Superficial stuff. I don't want to hear your cover story."

"You asked," Nancy replied wearily.

"What about your mom? Didn't get along with her, huh?"

"Actually, she died when I was three."

Michael rolled onto his back and stared up at the ceiling.

Nancy felt a strange awkwardness, as if the energy had been sucked out of the space between them. "It's okay. I don't mind talking about it."

Michael cleared his throat. "No, it's not that. It's just that . . ." He looked down at the hay and rubbed his temples.

"What's the matter, Michael?"

Michael shrugged. "My mom died, too, when I was six," he finally said.

Nancy glanced over at him. Michael's eyebrows were pulled together and his cocky expression had disappeared.

"You never really get over it, do you?" she asked.

"My dad tried to fill the space," Michael said quickly, trying to reclaim his wavering voice. He forced a laugh. "He married Debbie when I was eight, and that lasted two years. He married Marguerite when I was twelve. And shortly after that, he moved on to a series of short and meaningless relationships."

Michael chewed on a piece of hay. "I was pretty relieved when it came time to go to college."

"My dad never remarried."

"You're lucky."

"Yeah," she admitted. "But I never realized just how lucky until he had his first serious girlfriend—this year. Avery."

Michael gave her a wry smile. "You get a strange feeling of being a third wheel in your own home."

"I sure know that feeling," Nancy said. "Avery

made me feel as if I had *no* role in my own family. We've worked through some of that now, but still . . ."

She and Michael just looked at each other and nodded.

"I had a great nanny, though," Michael said.

"We had a housekeeper who was like a mom to me," Nancy said softly. "Her name is Hannah. She still takes care of things for my father."

Michael laced his fingers behind his neck. "Hey, Nancy, don't get nervous, but I just heard something."

"What?" Nancy was startled.

"I think I just heard us have a conversation." Michael's winning smile returned.

Nancy laughed, at first genuinely, but then awkwardly. When their eyes met, she turned away, holding back whatever she was thinking and feeling. It was true that Michael could be arrogant and condescending, but a small voice told her that there might be someone very different inside.

"Bring anything to eat?" Michael asked. "I bet you've hidden away a three-course meal for two and you're not telling me."

Nancy was grateful for the release of tension. She reached for her leather purse and dug inside it.

"One week-old granola bar," she said triumphantly, holding it up to view.

"You're a wizard." Michael took it and tore it open.

"Save me some," she commanded.

Nancy continued searching. "Here's a package of crackers and a tea bag." When she reached into her pocket and pulled out a pack of gum, a few slips of paper flew out with it.

"Not much here, but—" Nancy started to say, when one of the papers caught her eye. It was creased but still in one piece.

Nancy's heart pounded as she read the note on the large yellow sticky paper. "It's something I picked up off the floor at Jean-Marc's meeting last night. I was going to check it out right away, but I forgot. Michael, it's a list of tips for Money Plane recruiters."

Michael took the small piece of paper and read it out loud. " 'Tip Number One: Make your meetings fun and upbeat. Share stories of successful players and the fabulous things they did with their winnings. Tip Number Two: Never use the words *pyramid* or *scheme*. Give your meetings credibility by stressing that players are wise investors, not gamblers. Tip Number Three: For your protection, use a fun code name and demand cash payments. . . .' "

"Look at the bottom of the memo," Nancy said excitedly.

Michael squinted. "It's signed. Sort of. With the initials G.G. If we can just figure out who G.G. is, we might be onto something."

"Goldfinger," Nancy said. "This could be our link to Goldfinger."

CHAPTER 7

"If you don't stop, my sides are going to split." Ginny laughed as she ran down the single flight of stairs after Ricky. "Where are you taking me?"

Ricky pointed his flashlight into the basement and said, mock seriously, "Down."

They had reached the basement, and a smallish metal door appeared to their immediate right.

"Shhhhhh," Ricky whispered, slipping a key into the door's padlock while lowering his eyes mysteriously.

Ginny bopped him gently on the head with her flashlight. "This is too weird. You have a body buried down here or something?"

"If I did, I wouldn't tell you." Ricky cackled mysteriously.

"Thanks," Ginny said as they entered a narrow, cement-block hallway. She could still hear the sound of the howling blizzard, but down here it was muffled and blissfully quiet. Pipes and wires ran along the ceiling, and the air was balmy.

"The boiler room is that way"—Ricky pointed—"so it's nice and warm."

"This is creepy," Ginny said, her blood starting to fizz with excitement.

Ricky moved ahead. "You pre-med types can stomach blood, gore, and messy emergencies. All that's more frightening than a dark hallway."

"Actually, I spend most of my time with my organic chemistry textbook," Ginny explained.

Ricky turned and gave her a wry smile. He was cute, Ginny thought. Definitely cute. She liked his sense of adventure and quirky interests. In the semidarkness, he almost reminded her of Ray.

"Okay, check it out," Ricky was saying, pointing the beam of his flashlight ahead.

Ginny gasped. They were no longer in the Thayer Hall basement. They seemed to have entered some kind of underground tunnel. "Where does this go?" she asked.

"It used to lead from the building they tore down when they built Thayer, on the same foundation," Ricky explained. "I found the plans when I was doing research for class. There are tunnels all over the campus. Actually, all *under* the campus."

"That's incredible. What were they for?"

"To escape nuclear fallout," Ricky whispered, waving her ahead. "Come on."

Ginny shivered. "Oh, yeah. Back in the late

fifties, when everyone was worrying about nuclear attacks."

"They thought if they had a place to stuff people, they'd all survive," Ricky said, pointing to a series of wooden compartments along one side of the tunnel. "They even installed these storage areas for water, food, and blankets."

"Hold this," Ricky said, handing Ginny his flashlight. He opened one of the compartment doors.

Ginny's hand bumped his as they peered into the dusty space. Ricky's face was very close, and she could detect the spicy scent of his aftershave in the darkness.

"The tunnels connect all the major buildings on the campus," Ricky explained. "I got the key from one of the maintenance guys when I told them I was doing research on Wilder's original building plans. The girders supporting these tunnels were three-inch-thick steel."

Ginny followed until the tunnel turned at a right angle and ended at another door, which Ricky unlocked and pushed open. "Guess where we are."

"I recognize that smell," Ginny said.

"Ta-dah," Ricky said, unlocking and pushing open another door.

"The main campus cafeteria!" Ginny exclaimed. "And it's totally deserted."

Ricky ran his light up and down the well-stocked shelves and refrigerator doors. "No power. No food service staff. Just you, me, and enough food for three thousand people."

"I'm starved."

"Should we go hog-wild or be choosy?"

Ginny opened one of the big stainless steel re-frigerators. "Let's do both," she whispered. "Oooh. Ham. Roast beef. Cheese slices. A big sheet of those lemon crunch squares."

"I haven't eaten in six hours."

"Find the bread, mayonnaise, and mustard," Ginny ordered.

A few minutes later they were seated cross-legged on the cafeteria's big, steel serving counter with the sandwiches Ricky had made. Ginny lit a set of candles she'd found in the faculty din-ing room.

"Cheers." Ricky tipped his jug of chocolate milk and Ginny hoisted her own industrial-size container of apple juice.

Ricky looked even better in the candlelight, Ginny decided. He had a squarish face that dim-pled up when he talked. Plus, he was completely different from what she'd expected. She thought architecture majors were a mostly uptight, detail-oriented group. But Ricky had a fun, easygoing personality. She also liked it that he didn't talk only about sports and classes, like most guys she'd met since Ray.

"Let's take as much food as we can back to the dorm when we're done," Ginny said. "I'm beginning to feel guilty."

"I know. We're having too much fun."

Ginny laughed. "We're definitely not suffering enough to be in the middle of a blizzard."

Ricky held his sandwich in midair and looked at her. "I wish we had blizzards more often."

"Me, too, Ricky," Ginny heard herself saying back. "Me, too."

"We've shut down this road until further notice!" a uniformed trooper was hollering over the storm.

"I've got a plow on this truck!" Bess's driver yelled back, just as a gust of wind hit the side of the tractor.

Bess gripped the sides of her seat. Outside the truck, there was only darkness and whirling snow. For the past hour she and Hank—her snowplow lift—had crept along at a snail's pace behind a long line of cars. Bess's feet were frozen, and they were still nowhere near the Old Mill House, where Max was DJing the party.

"Sorry. Emergency vehicles only for the next six hours, at least."

Bess's heart sank.

Hank slumped over the steering wheel, then looked over at her with a smile. "That was the bad news."

Bess rubbed her arms. "Yeah, I guess so."

"The good news is that they stopped us right in front of the Dewdrop Truck Stop."

"Is that good?"

Hank stepped on the accelerator and pulled up in front of a huge, brightly lit structure, surrounded by cars and semis. "It's got the best coffee shop in the state. Cinnamon buns as big as your plate."

Bess perked up. "That's exactly what I need right now."

"Whew. It's crazy out here tonight." Hank whistled under his breath as they lumbered through the parking lot. "Lotta people wanted to go somewhere else pretty bad tonight."

"Yeah. And I'm one of them," Bess said sadly, wondering if Max was starting to worry about her. She sighed and looked over at Hank. Luckily, Hank was a really nice guy. He and his dad ran a large farm, located right across the highway from where Max was playing. Max had apparently flagged him down that afternoon, when he saw that Hank was headed back into town on his truck.

"Hey," Hank said, setting his brake and straightening his baseball cap. "Really sorry you can't meet your friend tonight. Seemed like a decent guy. He even offered to pay me to pick you up, but I turned him down. I was going into Weston for a part anyway."

Bess smiled. "Thanks, Hank."

Hank nodded toward the restaurant. "Let's go inside and warm up."

"Yeah. Maybe you can help me track down the phone number where Max's working," Bess suggested.

The Dewdrop was jammed. Weary-looking travelers were camped out on the floor of the carpeted entryway. Waitresses bustled around with pots of coffee, and the smell of steaks and pancakes filled the air.

Bess and Hank quickly headed for the bank of phone booths.

"Phones are out, honey," a waitress called out. "Storm knocked them out an hour ago."

"Oh, no," Bess moaned. She found an empty space against the wall and sank down.

"We're stuck here for a while," Hank sympathized, pulling off his big farm gloves and wiping his forehead. "Probably for the night."

"And no one knows where I am," Bess whispered.

"My van's not going anywhere," Cory called out, slamming the door behind him.

Ray picked out a few stray chords, then raised his head. Ever since he and Montana had come back from the Bumblebee, Cory had been on edge.

"What's wrong?" Montana asked, standing up.

Cory strode over to the wood stove, not looking at her. "It's sitting in two feet of snow, that's what's wrong."

Ray set down his guitar. "You want some help?"

Cory didn't answer. He sat down with a stony, distant expression as he held his hands up to the stove for warmth. Ray could see a muscle twitching in his jaw.

"I thought you and Montana were going to scrounge Weston for batteries," Karin said, sauntering over and snapping her gum.

Montana spoke before Cory could yell at Karin. "Let's look for some old boards, Cory," she said softly. "That'll help you get some traction."

"Forget it," Cory snapped. "Even if I could get it moving, I wouldn't be able to see the road. It's whiteout conditions."

Ray whistled. Then he checked his watch. "It's almost eleven."

Karin held two fists up in the air and threw her head back. "All right. We're stuck here, guys. There's no way around it."

Ray nodded. "Karin's right."

"Bummer," Montana groaned.

"I've got a couple of blankets in my trunk," Ray said, finding his jacket and pulling on a hat. "Cory, you've got two sleeping bags in the van, right?"

"Whatever you say, Ray," Cory said, giving him a dark look before walking toward the door.

Ray felt his stomach clench. So, Cory was angry he'd gone with Montana to the Bumblebee. Sure, they'd had a good time. And, yes, he was attracted to her. But it wasn't as if anything had happened between them. Why was Cory so bent out of shape?

Once outside, Ray bent his head into the blowing snow. He felt his arm being grabbed and twisted around.

"What are you doing, man?" Cory spat. Snow swirled into his eyes, but Cory just stood there, staring at Ray.

Ray looked down.

Cory reached out and nudged his arm. "Montana didn't get a minute of your time when she was falling all over you."

Ray wiped his face with the back of his glove. "Come on, Cory," he tried to reason. "Let's talk about this inside."

"No way!" Cory shouted, giving Ray a shove. "Montana and I get together and—boom—you're hitting on her."

"Montana and I are friends. She's the one who got this band together in the first place."

Cory's face was coated with ice and snow. "Forget it, Ray. I know how your mind works. Find someone else," Cory roared. "Montana and I are just starting something good. You don't have the right to mess with other people's lives, just because yours stinks."

Ray opened his mouth to say something, but he closed it and turned away. He stalked toward his car, wrapping his arms around his body for warmth. He was angry at Cory and confused about Montana. But he was suddenly sure about one thing.

He needed to talk to Ginny.

When Michael opened his eyes, his coat was frosted with snow. Bits of hay were stuck to his head. Sunlight was streaming in shafts through the barn ceiling and silence filled his ears. The roar of the wind was gone. The storm was over.

"Nancy?" he whispered.

Still asleep, she had shifted during the night so that she was now curled under the crook of his arm. He looked down, not daring to wake her. The pressure and warmth of her body next to his was making him light-headed.

Michael squeezed his eyes shut. What was going on? This was Nancy Drew, the girl who'd been making his life difficult. This was the girl who'd fouled up all his plans.

Still, Michael thought, there she was, asleep under a pile of hay, knowing things about him that he swore he'd never tell a soul. He shook his head, remembering how much they had confided in each other the night before.

"The problem we have, Nancy," Michael whispered, "is that we're too much alike."

Michael tried to tear his eyes away from the face asleep on the hay beside him, but they wouldn't move. He watched the gentle rise and fall of her chest. Her red-gold hair shimmering against her bare ear. The creamy curve of her cheek.

He bent down and breathed in the warm, sweet scent of her neck. Then he tenderly ran one finger along the edge of her jacket collar. He could actually feel her soft breath against his lips.

Michael had always prided himself on his self-control. Letting his guard down had never been an option for him. He could always hold out longer than his enemies and strike when they were at their weakest.

But at that moment, as he bent his lips down to Nancy's, he forgot everything but her beautiful face.

At first Nancy had only the sensation of a feathery warmth on her face. She forgot where she was until she took in the springy surface beneath her and the smell of hay.

Then she felt the slow movement of a hand brushing the side of her face, and her eyes flew open.

In a split second, she realized that she was staring at Michael's face, which was suspended only a few inches over her own. His eyes, soft and brown, were half-closed. His lips hovered, about to press on hers.

"Michael," she cried, yanking her head away and sitting up. "Stop it!"

"I—I . . ." Michael stammered, pulling up. He moved over and turned away in embarrassment.

Nancy could feel her face flush. "What were you doing?"

"Nothing," Michael said, swallowing.

Nancy knelt and brushed the hay off her coat. The memory of their long talk vaguely floated back, but she was still rattled.

There was a long silence, which Michael finally broke. "I wasn't doing anything. . . ." he began quietly.

"Yes, you were," Nancy snapped back before she realized how awful her voice sounded. "Whatever it was you were doing—you were definitely doing it."

Michael's eyes darkened. "Doing what?"

"You were all over me," Nancy flared, unable to stop herself.

Michael's face turned to stone. "Don't flatter yourself."

"I'm stating a fact."

Michael stood up, jammed his hands deep into his jacket pockets, and strode away. He leaned into the barn door and pushed it open a bare inch against the snow. Luckily the wind had cleared a patch in front of the door, making a drift off to the side.

Nancy watched Michael shake his head in the shaft of light that fell across him. As she began to pull her thoughts together, she realized she had made a big mistake. Sure, she'd instinctively pulled away from Michael. But it was the *old* Michael she'd seen.

There was a new Michael now, Nancy realized. The Michael who had opened up to her the night before. The Michael who understood her in a way no one ever had.

"I hear snowplows coming," Michael shouted back to her as a faraway rumbling began to fill the air. He hurried over and hoisted the video camera case over his shoulder. "I'm going to flag one down. You do what you want."

The new Michael had been about to kiss her, Nancy realized, as her heart began to thump in her rib cage. But now it was too late.

"Pam?" Will shouted into the phone.

"Hello? Will?" Pam Miller, George's roommate, mumbled.

"Is George back yet?" Will asked.

"Back?" Pam said. "I thought she was with you."

"George has been missing since yesterday morning. Where have you been?" Will said, feeling the knot tighten in his stomach.

Pam gasped. "I was with Jamal all day. We went to a party last night and I didn't get back until late."

Will pressed his hand to his forehead and sat down.

"George is missing? Her overnight bag is here," Pam said slowly. "But her cross-country skis are gone."

"Oh, no," Will murmured. "If she went skiing, then she must have been stranded somewhere all night."

"Oh, no." Pam's voice echoed Will's.

"Campus security hasn't found her," Will said, feeling his voice waver with panic. "I'm going out to look for her myself."

"Will," Pam shouted into the phone. "Don't hang up—"

But Will set the phone down, sick with fear. George. His George. She was tough. But how could she have survived a day and night like that?

"Sure—I'd go home—if I thought you really wanted me to, baby." The guy was breathing into Stephanie's ear.

"I want you to," Stephanie said frankly.

"Yeah, sure," he mumbled as they stepped off the elevator into the hall outside her suite. "All night long, you walked around the pool table giving me the eye. Oh, yeah, I could tell you really wanted me gone."

Stephanie closed her eyes in frustration. The guy was totally gorgeous, but there was no way she was going to do anything about it. Especially at eight o'clock in the morning. Oh, and she was married, too, Stephanie had to remind herself.

"It's been great—Dave. But it's dawn and I've got to go."

"Greg. My name is Greg," lover-boy said.

"Oh. Well, Greg, thanks. It was fun." Stephanie tried to slip in her door, but Greg put a hand on the frame and stopped her.

" 'It was fun,' " he mimicked her.

"Oh, please," Stephanie drawled. She was keeping her cool, but inside she was starting to get a little worried.

"Stephanie?" she heard a voice call from down

the hall. Dawn moved toward her, wrapped in her old blue bathrobe.

Stephanie smiled at Greg. "Remember Dawn Steiger from our pool game? She's my resident advisor."

"Everything okay?" Dawn asked quietly.

Greg gave them both a disgusted look, then turned to the elevator and punched the down button. The elevator hadn't left the floor, so the door opened immediately.

Stephanie breathed with relief when it closed again. "Thanks," she said.

"I come in handy, don't I?" Dawn responded, rather pleased with herself.

"Yeah, but it's pretty early on a Sunday morning to be roaming the halls, Dawn. What are you doing?"

"I've been trying to keep track of everyone during the storm. Everyone's accounted for, except Nancy."

Stephanie took out a cigarette. "Nancy? How could you possibly be concerned about Nancy?"

"Because she's unaccounted for and the wind-chill factor last night was thirty degrees below zero," Dawn said bluntly.

Stephanie sat on the lounge sofa and pulled off her boots, her cigarette dangling from her mouth. "If the world were coming to an end, Nancy Drew would be the one you'd turn to for flashlights, first-aid kits, and sensible advice. She's got Girl Scout preparedness embedded in her genetic structure."

Dawn shrugged. "I hope you're right."

"You'll see," Stephanie said as she stumbled to her old room. "Our Girl Scout will be back, bright and cheerful, soon enough."

Inside her room, Stephanie stubbed out her cigarette and slipped out of her clothes, which lay on the floor where they fell. Gratefully she sank into her rumpled bed. She was seconds away from drifting off to sleep when the phone rang.

"Steph?" A voice she knew came over the line.

"Jonathan?" Stephanie mumbled.

"Yeah, it's me, darling." Jonathan's voice seemed very far away. "Who else at this hour? I've been trying to reach you since last night."

Stephanie tensed. "Oh. It's been crazy with the storm and everything. The power's been out, and the phones haven't been working very well."

"Of course," Jonathan said with a laugh. "I hadn't thought of that."

I'm glad *I* thought of it, Stephanie said to herself. The last thing she needed was Jonathan finding out she'd been up all night with a guy named Greg. Or was it Dave?

"How's it going?" Stephanie managed to say before a mammoth yawn caught her.

"Great," Jonathan said enthusiastically. "I'm really psyched about this management training, Stephanie. They brought in this guy from New York who's a motivational expert."

"Oh," Stephanie said, climbing back into bed, trailing the phone cord. She let her eyelids drop as she nestled her head comfortably into her pillow.

"Employees are motivated when they believe

they have a stake in the organization, Steph," Jonathan was saying. "It's all about ownership of the product."

"Mmm."

"I want to use this concept with my department managers, Steph. . . ."

Jonathan's voice began to sound as if it were coming through a wad of cotton as sleep started to close over Stephanie.

"I think we can make great improvements, especially in housewares. . . ."

She vaguely felt the receiver drop from her hand, and then everything faded away as she fell into a deep sleep.

"I'm beginning to see the light," Ross laughed as he dug a canoe paddle into the snow drift.

George squinted into the wall of snow that covered the boathouse doorway. She could no longer see Ross, but could only hear him as he dug himself farther into the small tunnel he was cutting through the drift.

"Maybe we should just stay here until spring," George suggested.

Ross ducked his snowy head back inside and his eyes twinkled at her. "I'd love to, but I'm longing for ham and eggs—and coffee."

George hunted through a pile of lifejackets for the other paddle. "What's your hurry? We've only been buried alive for twenty-four hours."

"Yahoo." She heard Ross's muffled voice. "I broke through. The sun's shining out here."

George crawled through to reach him, and a moment later she was standing up in deep snow, her face bathed in sunlight.

The lake spread out before her, a sheet of unspoiled white snow. The deciduous trees were no more than silver poles against the blue sky. The evergreens were everwhites.

"Ahhhhhh." George tested her vocal cords happily and loudly. She spread her arms wide and stretched.

"You are like a sleepy mountain lioness coming out of hibernation," Ross said admiringly. Then he reached out with his canoe paddle and tapped her on the shoulder. "From this day forward, your guardian spirit shall be the mountain lion." He raised the paddle and touched her other shoulder. "I have spoken."

George pretended to fall from the paddle's gentle impact. The soft powder felt like a cloud. She looked up and stared at Ross, who was standing over her, grinning. George swallowed hard.

Ross wasn't just brilliant and completely fun, he was incredibly good-looking. He was wearing a trim, black polar fleece vest and very dark mountain climbing sunglasses. From this perspective, he looked vaguely like a friendly alien.

He reached down and grasped her hand, then pulled her up.

"Thanks," George said.

"Whoa," Ross said as her balance faltered.

She laughed as she tipped awkwardly to the

side, searching for a foothold in the deep snow. Suddenly, Ross's arm was around her waist, steadying her. Her chest brushed up against his and she found herself inches from his rugged face, looking straight into his eyes.

For a long moment George couldn't move. Ross's arm was as strong as an iron band, but his blue eyes were as soft and clear as the blue sky.

"George," Ross said quietly before he bent his head and dropped a long, tender kiss on her lips.

At first George felt as if she were falling through space, bathed in a celestial light. His kiss was like everything else about Ross Yaeger: certain, passionate, and very, very warm.

Then something clicked in George's mind: Will's face—worried, hurt, loving—as if he were watching them.

"No," George said abruptly, pulling away. She turned and crawled back down the short tunnel into the boathouse. Quickly she began to gather her things.

"George," she heard Ross say. "Come back out here. Please, I didn't mean to upset you."

"I know you didn't," George called out, trying to control her voice. "It's okay."

She heard him move back into their winter lair. Ross took her hand and turned her around to face him. He took her other hand and gazed at her seriously. "I know, you told me about Will. But, remember, we have nothing to be ashamed of. Nothing happened last night."

George hung her head. Why was she feeling so

sad suddenly? The feeling confused her. But what Ross said was true. They had huddled under their sailcloth blanket, talking until they both fell asleep, but there had been no physical romance. They had become close, though, in a very short time. Nothing had happened, but everything had changed.

"Look"—Ross took off his snowy gloves, and cupped her face in his hands, angling it slightly upward to look George full in the eye—"I know I'm a professor and you're a student and this shouldn't be happening."

"Nothing's happening," George whispered, lowering her chin so her gaze fell to the ground.

"Look at me," Ross said softly. "I'm not going to tiptoe around this. Something *is* happening, and I won't let you deny it. I feel very strongly about you, George."

George bit her lip. "Last night was fun," she said shyly.

Ross was scanning her face intently. George felt as though he were reading her mind. She tried to deny the truth that lay there—that she, too, felt very strongly about him.

Last night had been more than fun. It had been magical. They weren't just two people cheerfully putting up with the storm together—they were two people discovering each other.

"I know you can feel it, too, George," he said cautiously. "If you allow yourself to feel it."

Tears welled up in George's eyes; she couldn't will them away. "Feel what?"

"Don't do this, George," Ross pleaded. "Don't hide from me."

But George twisted out of his hold and picked up her skis, saying nothing but praying her awakening feelings for Ross would just go away. Will, she said to herself. Think Will.

"Don't deny this," Ross continued, his voice edged with pain. "It's too precious, George. It's so rare. Be honest with yourself—and me."

"Look," George said, turning around and planting her feet. "We've been stuck in a storm together, Ross. Real life stopped for a while, that's all. We've had twenty-four hours together in a dream. A very good dream."

"It wasn't a dream," Ross said firmly.

"*I* was dreaming," George said, raising her voice to keep it from trembling. "Now you're going back to work and I'm going back to classes and Will."

Ross's jaw tightened. A long silence, charged with electricity, settled between them. Then, so softly George could barely hear him, Ross said, "I understand."

"I'm in love with Will Blackfeather," George said out loud. "And there's nothing I can do about that."

As she watched Ross move away, George felt her heart squeeze with regret. Should she listen to her heart or her head?

Hi." A voice floated into Ginny's ear.

She cracked open one sleepy eye and gazed at the floor of the Thayer Hall lounge. Empty soda cans. Tomato-stained paper plates. Trampled cookies. Two brown shoes.

She managed to pry her other eye open, which gave her a little better perspective. She located her own feet, jammed against the arm of the sofa she was stretched out on. They wore shoes, so the two brown shoes she saw must belong to someone else.

She scanned her horizon until she found the brown shoes again. There were feet in them. Her eyes ran up to the ankles attached to the feet, the legs, the torso, and on up to the face at the top.

"Hi," the voice repeated.

Ginny focused. It was Ricky. "Hi," she mumbled. A rumbling wave crashed in her stomach. "Ugh. I ate too much late night. What time is it?"

Ricky looked at his watch. "Eight A.M., Sunday morning." He frowned. "You don't look so hot."

Ginny covered her face with her hands. "Thanks. What did we eat last night? No, wait. On second thought, I don't want to know."

After she and Ricky had returned through the tunnel with food, everyone had gone wild. Between games of pool and poker, they consumed a ten-pound tub of pretzels, twenty-five lemon squares, a three-by-two-foot baking sheet of cold lasagna, and a five-pound tin of Swedish butter cookies.

The last thing Ginny remembered was a massive game of Twister at three o'clock in the morning.

"Ginny?" Ricky was asking. "Is something wrong?"

"I think so," Ginny said, swinging her legs in slow-motion over the side of the couch. She sat more than a minute while her blood started flowing through her veins again. Ricky gallantly helped her stand up. Ginny mouthed the words "Thank you," and tried to smile. Ricky looked paler in the morning light than she remembered. "I need to get back to my room and recover," she said wearily.

"Okay," Ricky said, helping her step over the sleeping bodies. "Look, Ginny. There's an art exhibit opening tonight at Rand Hall. Would you like to go?"

Ricky waited for Ginny's reply, but all Ginny could do was stand there, looking at him. Finally she realized what was wrong. Ricky wasn't Ray.

She hadn't noticed until that moment that Ricky was actually much taller than Ray. And his jacket wasn't black. It was brown. His voice was higher and his speech was slower than Ray's.

"I can't," Ginny heard herself say.

"Oh." Ricky filled that one syllable with a lot of disappointment. "Okay."

"It's not that I didn't have a good time last night, Ricky. I did."

Ricky acted uncomfortable. "Hey. You're just busy tonight."

"No," Ginny said earnestly. "No, that's not it."

"Ginny, what's going on?"

"I'm sorry, Ricky," Ginny said as her thoughts straightened themselves out and formed a line. "I just figured something out, thanks to you. I do think you're great." She leaned forward and gave him a kiss on the cheek. "But I can't date you. I've got to go now. There's someone I need to get in touch with."

"I get it," Ricky said. Ginny could tell from his voice that it was true—he understood.

"Good luck," he said. "I'm glad I could help."

Ginny grinned. "You're great, Ricky. You're a great friend."

"Yeah, you, too," Ricky said, shaking his head sheepishly. "Now get going. You don't want him to get away."

"Thanks, Ricky," Ginny said, kissing him again on the cheek before hurrying out the door.

* * *

"Wait!" Nancy yelled at Michael as he staggered ahead of her through the waist-deep snow. Behind them, the barn roof was a barely visible wedge in the glittering snow field. On the road, a mammoth snowplow was shooting a huge plume of snow off the highway.

"Michael!" Nancy cried out, her eyes fixed on the flashing, yellow lights. "Flag that down."

"Here comes something else," Michael shouted back after not connecting with the plow.

Nancy finally made it up to the road and saw an orange-and-white van lumbering toward them. The sign on its hood read Grant County Medic One.

Nancy jumped into the road and waved her arms until it stopped.

"Hop in," the driver shouted, pointing to the back of the van. "I can take you to the nearest town."

"Thanks," Nancy shouted back. "We've been stranded here all night."

They swung into the back of the ambulance, where a rather burly woman was moving some equipment off a cot.

"Sit down," she called out as the ambulance began moving. She took a seat on a chair just behind the driver and grinned at them. "We've got a possible cardiac arrest in Braemer. Take you that far if you want. Lose your skis?"

"Our car went off the road last night," Nancy explained. "We camped in that barn back there."

The medic noticed blood oozing from the cut

on Michael's forehead. She took a small flashlight from the pocket of her white jacket. "Better let me take a look at that."

"Are you okay, Michael?" Nancy asked quietly.

"I'm fine," Michael said, not looking at her. "Maybe a little out of my mind, but nothing more."

The medic chuckled and pulled something out of a drawer. "Who isn't?"

Michael pointed his thumb at Nancy. "Well, *she* believes she's perfectly sane."

The medic laughed. "Then she probably is."

Nancy appreciated the medic's support.

"I think you could use some stitches, but I can't give them to you here and we won't be going back to the hospital for some time," the medic said. "I'm afraid you're out of luck in any case."

"What do you mean?" asked Michael a little nervously.

"There's only a certain window of time during which stitches will help," she explained. "If this happened last night, you're probably too late. The wound has already started healing."

"So what does that mean in terms of the wound?" asked Nancy.

"I'm going to clean it and get a bandage on it." She started getting out her supplies. "It will heal okay—though you must watch for signs of infection you might have picked up since it happened. Hopefully, I'll get that all out now."

"That's not so bad," Michael said. "In that case, why would anyone ever get stitches?"

The medic paused for a moment, then looked at Nancy. "Is your boyfriend vain?"

Nancy flushed and felt flustered. What do I say about the boyfriend? she wondered.

"Vain? Is Michael vain?" Nancy started chuckling a little uncontrollably. Between breaths, she managed to say, "Yes, he's vain."

Michael shot her an evil look.

"Well, you are—*dear*," she said, playing the part of the girlfriend.

"In that case—" the medic began, but she was interrupted by a howl of pain from the patient. "Oh, yes, sorry. This procedure is likely to hurt a little. Got to get all that possible infection out. Anyway, as I was saying, without stitches, you're going to have a doozy of a scar."

Michael groaned. "Please, can you just finish cleaning it and stop talking about it?"

Nancy volunteered a change of subject. "What's in Braemer?" she asked the medic. "Would it have a car rental agency?"

The medic dabbed Michael's forehead with wet gauze. "Nope."

Nancy's heart sank.

"Braemer is an outpost for local farmers," she explained. "You've got your country store and the infamous Dewdrop Truck Stop."

Michael winced as the woman applied medicine with a cotton swab. "We're trying to get back to Wilder University."

The medic whistled. "Tough break. The highway between Braemer and Weston is still closed to everything but emergency vehicles."

Michael looked down at the video camera case. "Guess we can kiss our interview good-bye for this week."

"The story still stands," Nancy reasoned. "We'll do it next week."

"Next week the Money Plane will be ancient history," Michael snapped. "The *Wilder Times* will have written the story to death by then."

Nancy straightened. "But we might . . ."

"Work with me on this, Nancy," Michael said sarcastically. "First, how are we going to get back to campus? We'll be lucky to make it home today at all. Say we do. Monday and Tuesday we edit this tape, write the script, finish the research and voice-overs and be ready by Wednesday afternoon? Plus schoolwork?"

Nancy knew he was right. And she also knew that she'd hurt him.

"Something will work out," Nancy said quietly, as the ambulance swayed down the snowy highway.

When she looked across at Michael, all the warmth was drained from his face. She wanted to tell him she was sorry. She wanted to tell him how crazy and mixed-up he was making her feel. But for right then at least, Michael could have been sitting a thousand miles away from her.

"Cory?" Montana called out softly.

She sat up in her sleeping bag and rubbed her

eyes. Ray, Karin, and Austin were still asleep on the floor around the woodstove. But Cory was already up, standing next to the window, softly picking out a tune on his guitar.

"Cory?" she whispered again. She pulled her sweater over her head and moved toward him.

Cory glanced back at her, then turned back to stare out the window. "The storm is over."

Montana bit her lip and stared. The morning sunlight fell in a square patch on the wooden floor. Outside, a row of icicles glistened. "Yeah. It's beautiful out there now."

Unexpectedly, Montana felt the pressure of tears. "Cory—I—"

"Forget it."

There was something very painful about staring at Cory's back. Montana realized—maybe for the first time—how much she cared about him.

She moved a step closer to him, so that her face was inches from his broad shoulder. "It's true," Montana said quietly. "I did have a thing for Ray."

Cory turned, just enough for her to see the anger in his eyes. "Tell me about it."

"But things are different now," Montana began.

Cory slipped his guitar strap off his shoulder and turned. "I told you, Montana. If you don't want this, then all you have to say is no. Don't say yes when you really mean no. Don't say maybe when you mean never. Don't say I'll tell you later when you know right now."

"Cory . . ." Montana couldn't believe Cory was acting this way.

He put his jacket on, packed his guitar in his case and closed it. "I really don't need this."

Montana's eyes flooded with tears as she watched him leave. Cory. How could she have been so thoughtless yesterday—carrying on with Ray? She knew Cory was sensitive. That was why she liked him so much.

Montana bent her head. Finally she'd found a guy she really wanted to be with—and who wanted to be with her.

It was amazing how quickly she'd let it slip through her fingers.

The floor of the Dewdrop lobby. The vinyl couch in the ladies' lounge. The horseshoe booth in the smoking section. Bess had slept in all three places by the time the sun rose through the windows of the restaurant. Her skin felt sticky, and her eyelids drooped with fatigue.

"More coffee?" the waitress asked.

"Keep it coming." Hank slid his cup over.

"Definitely," Bess agreed with a sigh, digging into her second piece of ham. The highway was still closed, but luckily, Hank had turned out to be a friendly guy who knew everything there was to know about making the perfect hamburger, classic cars, and James Bond movies.

Plus, the Dewdrop had food, and lots of it.

"Anyway," Hank was saying, "we usually plant about two thousand acres of corn."

"That's amazing," Bess said, putting her fork down. Hank helped run his family's farm.

He adjusted his cap and grinned. "Yeah. Well, we have lots of machinery and hire a lot of people at harvest."

Bess was smiling back and buttering her toast when she heard a familiar voice behind her.

"What about that huge booth over there?" the voice said. "There are only two people in it."

"Nancy?" Bess said to herself, turning around.

She gasped. Nancy and Michael were standing next to the cashier, arguing with each other.

"Hey, Nancy." Bess waved them over. "What are you doing here?"

"What are *you* doing here?" Nancy exclaimed as she walked toward her friend.

Bess's eyes grew wider by the second as Nancy headed down the aisle. She was wearing a plaid jacket, but it was smudged with mud and the right sleeve had a long tear. Her red-blond hair looked as if it had once been in a ponytail, but then had been clawed apart by small birds.

Bess stood up slowly. "What happened?"

"Oh," Nancy said wearily, her face pale and frozen. "Michael and I were in a car accident."

"Oh, my . . . Nancy," Bess exclaimed.

"We're okay. We found an old barn to stay in overnight, then this morning we got a ride, and here we are," Nancy explained. She rolled her eyes and turned away when Michael sat down next to her.

"Hi, Bess," Michael mumbled, hoisting his

black camera case into the booth. His forehead was bandaged, his jacket was soaked, and there were small bruises covering his hands.

"What were you doing on the road way out here?" Bess asked, sitting down slowly.

Nancy helped herself to Bess's water glass and took a long, shaky drink. "We drove over to Brockton College yesterday to interview a bunch of students who'd been ripped off by the Money Plane."

"Ripped off?" Bess cringed.

Michael leaned back while the waitress filled his coffee cup. "So we started driving back through the most incredible snowstorm—"

Nancy let her head rest against the back of the booth. "It was a whiteout. Couldn't see a thing."

"So, anyway," Michael said angrily, "if I may be allowed to continue uninterrupted . . . I'm turning around to get back to a gas station."

"I had to beg him," Nancy broke in.

"And Nancy starts shouting—"

"He didn't see the bend in the road—"

"She startles me. We spin out. And my bug leaves the road."

Bess covered her mouth with her hands.

"Then Michael insisted on stumbling blindly down the road in search of I don't know what. . . ."

"Stop!" Bess finally cried. "Chill out. Start way back. And this time, I'll be referee. What's this about the Money Plane turning into a rip-off at Brockton?"

Nancy shrugged. "It's true. We interviewed a woman whose Money Plane contact was the same guy who sold passenger seats with Jean-Marc last night—I mean, the night before last."

Bess bit her lip. "I don't believe it. Jean-Marc wouldn't get mixed up with someone like that."

Michael rubbed his eyes. "Jean-Marc was there in the thick of it. We have film."

Bess felt her blood starting to boil. "Listen, Michael, I know Jean-Marc. He would never even *think* about doing anything that would hurt anyone. Especially his friends. You theory is totally outrageous and crazy. And you should know better, Nancy."

"Bess!" Nancy cried out as Bess jumped up and headed for the phones.

"I'm going to call Eileen right now," Bess called back. "Maybe she knows something about this Ace." Tears began to flood her eyes. "I don't know how she's going to stay in the Kappas without any dues money, much less stay in school!"

CHAPTER 10

A half-hour later Michael was sitting alone in the booth, staring at the leftover outer ring of Nancy's cinnamon bun. He shut his eyes to stop the spinning in his head. Was it the blow from the accident? His frustration over the snow? Or the crazy way Nancy was making him feel?

Nancy, Bess, and Hank had left to make phone calls. The lines were so long, the waitresses had to start a number system.

The highway was still closed, so his prize interview sat in the camera case next to him, nothing but dead weight.

Michael raked his hair back with two hands. When Nancy wasn't right in front of him, he found himself longing for her. The lovely curve of her face. The quick, self-assured way she moved. The uncanny habit she had of reading his mind.

"Yet if she sat down in front of me right now,"

Michael muttered to himself, "I'd probably want to strangle her within two minutes."

He made a fist. If only he hadn't been so tempted to kiss her. "She's probably laughing at me right now," Michael whispered. He glanced over at the counter, where Bess and Nancy were having a lively conversation with Hank while waiting for their numbers to be called.

Michael broke off a piece of Nancy's cinnamon bun and ate it. Still, he believed that Nancy felt the same way about him. He had seen her feeling for him flash in her eyes enough that he knew it was there. Next time it would be Nancy who was unable to resist kissing him.

By the time Nancy, Bess, and Hank returned to the table, Michael was back in control. More snowbound travelers were coming through the Dewdrop's front door. Big lines had formed at the cashier and around the bathroom doors.

Michael began staring at a baseball cap—an ordinary cap on an ordinary middle-aged stranger.

"I see it, too," Nancy's voice interrupted his thoughts. "That's just like the gray cap—"

"That Ace was wearing at Jean-Marc's Money Plane meeting," Michael finished her sentence. "With the bluebird on it."

"Come on," Nancy said, standing and snaking her way through the crowd.

Michael hurried after her.

"Excuse me?" Nancy tapped on the man's shoulder. He was tall and wore farm overalls.

He turned around while sipping from an insulated cup. "Hi, there."

"Hi," Nancy greeted him. "I'm curious where you got your hat."

He took his hat off and looked at it along with Nancy and Michael. "At Braemer Stadium, where else? I'm a Blue Jays fan."

"Thanks," Nancy said.

"It cost six ninety-nine," the man continued.

"Thanks," Nancy repeated.

A woman standing near them volunteered that Blue Jays caps could be bought at the Braemer Country Store.

"Are you a Blue Jays fan?" Nancy asked Hank after they hurried back to the table.

"Sure, the Blue Jays are a big deal," Hank told them. "Everyone out here is crazy about baseball, and the Blue Jays' owner puts on a great show."

"Ace must be a local," Nancy reasoned, drumming her fingers on the table. "Unless he picked up the hat at Wilder or Brockton."

Hank shook his head. "The Blue Jays don't attract much of a college crowd. You guys have all that intramural stuff going on. We can't compete."

Michael drummed his fingers on the table. "If he's from around here, there must be someone who can identify him."

"I know who could do it," Hank said slowly. "Ollie Gilchrist. He owns the Braemer Country Store. He knows everyone in town."

"Take us over there, will you, Hank?" Michael asked. "We've got something important we need to ask him."

"As soon as the road's clear," Hank said. "No sweat."

"Come on, wake up, Steph," Casey, Stephanie's roommate, was calling out from her dorm door. "Get up, lazybones! It's past three in the afternoon."

Stephanie opened her eyes. Bright sunshine streamed in through the window.

Last night, she thought. Last night had been a total fiasco. There she'd been, ready to party, and the hunk she'd wanted had tiptoed away with Ginny Yuen.

Do I look married? Stephanie worried. Did I get older-looking? Is the whole marriage thing making me seem washed-out and boring?

Casey stuck her head in the door again. "There's a big ice-sculpture contest going on outside. I'll meet you down there."

Stephanie swung her legs out of bed and hurried to the window. Her cheeks warmed with excitement.

"Be there in a sec," Stephanie yelled.

Fifteen minutes later she was bursting out of Thayer Hall's big front glass doors into the glaring sunlight. Everyone was there. The front of the dorm looked like a cross between a snow carnival, a winter Olympic ski party, and a Saint Moritz art festival.

Fat-bellied snowmen stood along the border of the stairway. Scores of snow-encrusted students were building two massive snow forts for a war-like face-off, and scattered in the clotted snow field were at least a dozen intricate snow sculptures.

"Hey, Stephanie," a six-foot guy from her history class called out.

"Ahhhh!" Stephanie squealed as he threw a snowball from behind his fort. Without missing a beat, she scooped up a pile of snow and threw it back.

"You're artistic, Stephanie. Come on and help with our snow angel," Dawn shouted. She and Eileen were using plastic picnic knives to sculpt a five-foot-tall figure.

"Sure," Stephanie called out, bounding forward and doing a sudden cartwheel in the snow. "I'll do the wings.

"Yahoo!" she shouted to no one in particular. There were so many people outside that she doubted if anyone noticed how crazy she was acting—and how wonderful she felt.

She flashed on a hundred vacations she'd taken with her father—from the cruises to Mexico to the ski trips to Colorado. She'd loved those trips. They'd made her feel so carefree and happy. Right now everything in her life with Jonathan seemed so purposeful and serious.

Maybe I'm not ready to give up being a kid, Stephanie thought.

True, she had wanted to get married. She'd

started to get worried about her short attention span with men. She'd longed for someone she could count on, someone who wouldn't leave, and that someone had been Jonathan. Stephanie thought marriage would magically change her into the grown woman she wanted to be.

A deeply tanned guy in a red down jacket handed her a cup of steaming cider. "Nice cartwheel." He grinned. "What are you doing tonight?"

Stephanie winked at him, basking in the attention and the warm sun on her face but said nothing. She was bounding over to her snow sculpture when she heard Casey calling her.

"Stephanie, it's Jonathan."

Stephanie felt her stomach dip. "Jonathan?"

"Yeah! He's on the phone right now!"

"He just called me seven hours ago," Stephanie muttered under her breath.

"Hi, Jonathan," she panted, when she finally got back up to her room."

"Good news, Steph," Jonathan said. "The seminar is over early, and the Weston highway has just been opened."

Stephanie felt something pop in her heart, then sink slowly into her stomach. "You're coming—back?"

"Yeah," Jonathan said. "Tonight."

"Tonight."

"That's right. And you won't have to stay in that noisy dorm any longer."

"Right."

"Wait up for me. I'll pick you up at the dorm."

"Okay," Stephanie whispered, slowly dropping the receiver as the image of their tiny, shabby apartment flashed at her. She thought about the walls that pressed in on her like those of a prison.

"The State Patrol has reopened the highway," someone shouted through the front door of the Dewdrop Truck Stop.

Bess raised two victory fists as the crowd began to pour out through the front doors. "Whoo-ee!" she yelled like a cowboy.

"We're outta here!" Michael shouted.

Hank, who was pulling on his plaid farm coat, pointed to Bess. "Okay. You need to get over to the Old Mill House to see your boyfriend."

Bess nodded, flushing pink.

"Is it all right if we drop Michael and Nancy off on the way, so they can talk with Ollie?"

"Sure."

"Thanks, Hank," Nancy said. "Thanks, Bess."

"Round 'em up!" yelled Hank.

The parking lot was beginning to thin out, and several eighteen-wheelers were warming up their engines, sending clouds of steamy exhaust into the air. The snowplows had passed through again, leaving seven-foot-high snow embankments. State troopers were out in full force, waving cars, semis, and pickups back onto the road.

Nancy, Michael, and Bess squeezed together in the front seat of Hank's pickup with the plow attached. Fifteen minutes later Hank pulled up to the store. Nancy and Michael slipped out, and Bess rolled down the window to say good-bye.

"Thanks so much, Hank," Nancy said, sticking her head back inside. She turned to Bess. "I don't know how long we'll be, so don't worry about us. We'll hitch a ride back to campus."

"If Max and I see you, we'll stop," Bess said gaily, waving as Hank pulled away.

Bess hung on to the window frame to keep from being bounced out of her seat. "They may have had great cinnamon buns, but I'm really glad to be out of that truck stop," she told Hank.

"I understand that," Hank said. "Glad I could help."

A few minutes later Bess saw the Old Mill House's sign ahead, pointing to a barnlike structure. She hadn't been able to reach Max on the phone and had no idea if he'd still be waiting for her.

She told herself to relax. After all, she barely knew him. All Max was to her was a sweet guy who wanted to ask her out.

"I'll wait while you see if he's here," Hank said, giving her a thumbs-up. She hopped out and ran toward the building.

When she got to the barn doors, Bess heard loud voices and the squeak of a partly disconnected sound system. Inside, chairs were scattered about the empty dance floor, and a few people were moving sound equipment from the stage.

"Bess," Max's voice called from somewhere across the room.

"Hey—your girlfriend finally made it, Ridgefield," another voice called out.

Bess turned crimson as she saw Max approach her. She wasn't his girlfriend, really. And yet that's what Max must have told the people there.

Bess locked her eyes on Max's. It felt good—very good—to have someone call her Max's girlfriend. As he walked up to her, the exhaustion from her night seemed to rise up like a dark cloud and float away.

"I can't believe you're here," Max said. "I didn't know if you'd decided to stay home, or if you were stranded as we've been."

Bess took a good look at him, his short, blond hair, his black shirt, his broad shoulders, the worn brass buckle on the belt. She felt her heart stir as he took her hand and held it.

"Hank and I got as far as the Dewdrop Truck Stop last night," Bess explained. "Then we got stuck."

Max smiled and Bess smiled back, feeling the ties between them suddenly get stronger, even though none of their plans had worked out.

"My car's here," Max said shyly. "We can drive home as soon as I get my stuff packed up."

"Wait," Bess said, suddenly gripping his hand.

"What?" he asked.

"After all I went through to get here, do you think I'm going to turn back without one dance?"

Max grinned. "You want to dance?"

"Yes. I'd like that very much."

Max walked to the front of the dance floor, where his sound system was still hooked up. He pushed a tape into a machine, and a slow, melodic song filled the air.

Max turned, walked back toward her, and took her hand. Slowly, happily, Bess began to move to the music. A soft morning light broke through a window, and a moment later Max slipped an arm around her waist.

Their bodies were barely touching, but it seemed to Bess that they were very, very close. Closer than she'd been to anyone in a long time.

CHAPTER 11

I'm in love with Will Blackfeather, and there's nothing I can do about that, Ross. . . .Nothing I can do . . . Nothing I can do . . .

George kicked her skis ahead in the deep powder. Bright sunshine bounced off every crystal of glittering white. The blue sky seemed to lift her in the air.

She circled back around the lake toward campus, taking in the snowy woods, memorizing every detail. An hour ago she'd said good-bye to Ross and watched as he snowshoed back toward campus alone. She was wet, tired, and hungry, but she wanted to make sure she'd never forget this snowy spot by the lake and the way Ross Yaeger had made her feel.

A painful tightness gathered in her chest. Ross had wanted to see her again, but she'd refused. Now she imagined not seeing him for days and weeks. She pictured seeing him walk across campus and wanting to stop him.

She hated the idea of not being close to Ross when she returned to campus. And yet, how could she be? Right now she was committed to Will. Right now, she thought, but forever?

Plus, she had to be realistic. She was a student, and Ross was a professor. Relationships like that rarely worked out. There was the age difference. She was just starting her life, and Ross had already launched his career. That kind of imbalance was probably a recipe for disaster.

Besides, faculty-student romances were frowned upon at Wilder, and probably every other campus in the country. Ross could get in big trouble if he got involved with her. Not to mention what it might do to her reputation on campus.

George headed through a patch of woods and got her first glimpse of the snow-shrouded academic buildings since the day before.

"I have to see you again, George."

The Wilder buildings were lined up like white cakes around the campus lawn. She skied past them all.

"I don't know what I'm doing, Ross."

The street to Will's apartment was quiet. After releasing her boots from her skis, George climbed up the driveway to Will's apartment.

"George!" Will cried as he flung open the door to the kitchen.

"I'm okay," George said quietly as he pulled her inside and held her tightly.

"Andy, Reva," he called into the living room. "George is here!" They came running.

"What happened?" Will cried out, pulling away to look at her. His dark eyes took her in.

"I'll call the campus police and tell them she's okay," Reva said quickly. "You are okay, aren't you?"

George nodded. Reva pulled Andy back into the living room with her, saying, "I think they might want to be alone."

Will brushed the snow off George. "Did you get lost . . . did you . . ."

"I wanted to go for a short cross-country ski before you picked me up for our trip," George started to explain as she sank down into a kitchen chair.

Will pulled up a chair right next to hers and sat down. "George, the snow was coming down like crazy."

"Not when I started," George said simply. "It was so beautiful that I just wanted to be outside in the middle of it."

"Where did you go?" Will wanted to know.

"I went on that trail around the lake. . . ."

Will snapped his fingers. "The lake. I should have known."

"I was halfway around when the wind really picked up."

"You must be freezing," Will was saying, tenderly unzipping her jacket and pulling it off. "It's warmer in the living room." He made her sit down on the couch in the spot that Reva had just vacated.

"Well?" Reva planted a hand on her hip as she stood in front of George. "Where were you last night while we were here pacing the floor?"

George pulled off her boots and rubbed her frozen toes. "The only reason I'm not lying out there like a Popsicle is because I happened to bump into the university boathouse during the worst of the blizzard."

"You spent the night alone in the boathouse?" Will asked with alarm in his eyes. "You must be frozen."

George paused. She didn't have anything to hide, did she? "Actually, a guy named Ross Yaeger was stranded there, too. He'd been snow-shoeing. Luckily, the boathouse had a propane heater."

Reva gasped. Her eyes darted briefly toward Will's face, then back to George's. "You were stranded all night in a deserted boathouse with Ross Yaeger? *The* Ross Yaeger?"

Will frowned. "Who's he?"

George shrugged. "He's on the faculty of the English Department. Really nice guy."

Reva whistled. "Nice? He's totally gorgeous and single. *Famously* gorgeous and single."

Will cleared his throat. "What's that supposed to mean, Reva?"

"Oh, stop it," George said lightly, slipping an arm around Will's waist.

Reva raised one eyebrow. "Nothing happened that you want to tell us all about?"

Will stared at her.

Only everything, George thought.

"You up for this walk?" Ray asked Montana. He pulled his hat farther down on his ears, then dug his hands deep into the pockets of his leather jacket.

Weston's side roads were still buried in snow. Cory had made it out earlier, with boards for traction, but Ray and Montana decided to leave their cars and walk back to campus.

Montana nodded. "Sure. I've got a radio show to do. No choice."

Ray looked at her again. Her clear blue eyes were puffy.

"Are you okay, Montana?"

"Don't be a fool, Ray," Montana said softly. "You know what's going on."

Ray stopped walking. "Look, Montana. I'm sorry about all this. Honestly, I have no idea what's going on."

"You know what, Ray?" Montana said carefully. "I don't even care what's going on here— between you and me, that is. Because there is no you and me. I made a mistake thinking there ever could be."

"Yeah," Ray said, rubbing the back of his neck. "I did, too."

Montana stopped walking. Her curly blond hair shifted across her face, but she looked at him steadily. "I was hung up on you for a long time, Ray. That's why this is so hard for me."

Ray bit his lip.

"But it's Cory I care about now," she said with an earnestness he'd never heard from her before. "And I think he cares about me, too. And we want to be together."

"Believe me, I know." Ray kicked at the snow as he walked, head down.

"I wanted to be close to you yesterday," Montana admitted, rubbing her arms as her teeth began to chatter. "But I don't want it to happen again. I think you only want what you can't have these days."

Ray breathed in deeply. "Hey, aren't musicians supposed to struggle and suffer. That's how great love songs are written." Suddenly his mind flashed on Ginny.

Montana's expression was still serious. "I hurt Cory. We both did."

Ray took Montana's slender shoulders. "I can't afford to lose you or Cory as friends."

Montana's eyes softened. A smile began to form on her face. "Good."

He leaned in to kiss her on the cheek and felt nothing beyond friendship for her—no spark. It was only a nice feeling of comfort. There was no comparison to the way he felt when he was close to Ginny. Now, *that* was chemistry.

"Come on," Ray said, bending down to grab a handful of snow. "If you don't start moving, I'm going to drop this right down your neck."

Montana took off and packed a snowball of her own, which she lofted back at him.

Ray shook his head. She was right, he hadn't had any interest in her when she was available. Maybe the storm and the isolation had done something to his head. Or maybe it was because he missed Ginny so much he needed to put his arms around someone—anyone—for a few minutes.

Now here she was, Ray thought with a laugh, dumping *him*.

Ray and Montana trudged ahead and turned right on snowbound Main Street, where they strolled past the shops and restaurants that led toward the campus.

It felt good not to be walking alone, Ray thought. Maybe it had been loneliness that had made him see something in Montana that didn't exist.

Ray felt a stirring inside, and knew that Ginny had never really left his heart and probably never would. The longing inside wasn't going to go away unless he took action.

Now he knew what it was he had to do. He had to find Ginny. Soon.

Nancy's eyes opened wide as she and Michael entered the Braemer Country Store. Shelves ran from floor to ceiling on each side of the long room.

A checkout counter stood at the front, where

a large man in a plaid shirt was laughing with a customer.

"So Frank Watson had to *walk* to the Dewdrop through the blizzard?" He chuckled.

"Because Shirley ran out of coffee," the other man said, slapping his hand down.

"Uh, excuse me," Michael broke in, walking up. "My name's Michael Gianelli from Wilder University, and this is my friend, Nancy . . ."

"So, you must be the two kids who camped out in the old Larsson barn last night," the man behind the counter said instantly, extending his hand. "Name's Ollie Gilchrist. Glad to meet you. This here is Johnny Beemer."

"Hey," Johnny said, "that must be your Volkswagen bug down the road that's hugged up to that tree."

Nancy and Michael smiled and shook the men's hands. "How did you know who we were?" Nancy asked.

"People around here just keep an eye out," Johnny replied with a sly smile. "I'll bet it was mighty cozy in that barn while you two waited out the storm."

"It was actually pretty cold." Nancy blushed.

Michael laughed nervously and stuck his hands in his pockets. "You seem to have a nose for reporting. Would you like to come back with us to Wilder University? We've got a news show there," he joked.

The two men chuckled.

"Some other folks just south of town ran out

of gas during the storm and nearly froze to death on the highway. You two should consider yourselves lucky, finding that barn," Ollie said, leaning onto his elbows.

"Mr. Gilchrist?" Nancy asked. "Would you help us find someone?"

Ollie's eyebrows went up. "Are you in some kind of trouble?"

"Not exactly," Nancy said. "But we could prevent some people from getting in trouble if we can find this guy."

"We're looking for a guy—maybe twenty years old, tall with curly red hair—who lives around here," Michael said.

"He's a Blue Jays fan," Nancy added. "He wears the team cap."

Ollie planted both hands on his counter and pursed his lips thoughtfully. "College kid?"

"He could be," Nancy said.

Ollie gave them a suspicious look. "What's he done?"

"We'll let you know, Mr. Gilchrist, if we can verify that our information is correct," Michael said.

Ollie scratched his chin. "There's a family out this way. Big soybean operation. Name's O'Rourke, and every single one of them's got red hair."

"Do they have a son college age?" Nancy asked, trying to remain patient.

"Yep. Big John went off to college—Wilder, I believe," Ollie explained. "He's the middle one. Tall fellow. Played basketball for Central Valley

High. Forward. His little brother Allen is playing this year, as a matter of fact. He got a great game from outside. . . ."

"I'll be right back," Nancy whispered to Michael.

Nancy hurried outside, where she'd seen a pay phone. Finally, there was something she could do. It was the first sane moment she'd had in hours.

"Wilder University?" Nancy said into the phone. "I'm trying to track down a student named John O'Rourke. Do you have anyone in the dorms by that name?"

"One moment, please," the university operator said. "John O-R-O-U-R-K-E. We have someone by that name in Owens Hall."

Nancy eagerly wrote down the phone number and hung up. At last they were getting somewhere. They might have found Ace.

And if they found Ace, Goldfinger might be right behind him.

"Oh, man," Jonathan groaned, walking up the stairs to their off-campus apartment Sunday night. "It's good to be home. I'm beat."

Stephanie frowned at her watch. "It's only nine P.M., Jonathan."

"A long drive on treacherous roads will do that to you," Jonathan said, smiling over his shoulder as he unlocked the door.

Stephanie followed him inside and set her overnight bag on the kitchen dinette table. An empty container of yogurt and a cereal-studded bowl stood where she'd left them days ago. Newspapers were stacked up on the TV, and the whole place had a funny smell that reminded her of wet socks.

Jonathan turned around and slipped his hands around her waist. "Hello."

Stephanie stood up on tiptoe and kissed him. She looked affectionately at the broad curve of his shoulders and his thick, chestnut hair. She remembered how she used to swoon every time she looked at him like this. Now she could tell the feeling was something different, but she wasn't sure what.

She wrapped her arms around his neck, telling herself that the old spark would come back. He'd just been away for too long.

"Have fun?" Jonathan's gray eyes searched hers.

Stephanie grinned and pulled away. "A blast. It was so much fun to—you know—to see the old crowd again."

Jonathan opened the refrigerator door and pulled out a soda. Then he loosened his tie. "Chicago was great, Steph. I'm pumped about using all the sales training techniques I learned at Berrigan's—starting tomorrow."

"Really? That's great, honey," Stephanie forced herself to say. She had spent her weekend having fun and partying at a snowed-in, blacked-out college campus, and all Jonathan wanted to talk about were sales techniques. Was he always this boring? she thought sadly.

"You know what I want to do?" Jonathan asked, collapsing onto a worn cushion of their old brown couch. "I'm going to shoot for the store manager position right here at the Weston branch. It should be vacant in a couple of years."

"A couple of years?" she asked.

"Yep. That's when old Bill Brannon retires," he explained, but Stephanie wasn't interested in his reasoning. All she knew was that they needed to get out of this town and lifestyle and bring some excitement into their marriage. Even the room they were in felt like a cage at the moment.

Stephanie stood in the middle of the room in silence. She took in their old couch and the chipped Formica top of their kitchen table. Then she looked at Jonathan and tried not to get upset.

"Jonathan," Stephanie heard herself say tenderly. So far so good. "We didn't talk about that."

Jonathan rubbed his eyes. "About what?"

"About staying in Weston," Stephanie said quietly. "We were going to get·away—maybe New York."

Jonathan closed his eyes and nodded. "Yeah, I know. But it's just not going to happen fast, Steph. And you've still got your degree to get."

Stephanie walked over to the dinette table and sank down. Then she buried her face in her hands.

"What's wrong, darling?" Jonathan said softly. Stephanie felt her face go hot and her eyes swell with unexpected tears. "I don't know if I can do this."

"Do what?"

Stephanie slowly raised her head as Jonathan sat down across from her and folded his hands. "You look tired, Steph," he said.

She shook her head. "No, Jonathan. It's just that I've had a lot of time to think."

Stephanie saw that Jonathan was scared of what she might say. It was obvious to him that a serious talk was coming.

"Thinking goes on in the dorms?" he tried to joke.

Stephanie smiled weakly and took his hand. "I'm not ready for this, Jonathan."

She watched his face fall, as if she'd slapped it. "For what?" he asked.

Stephanie thought he probably knew the answer. "For marriage," she whispered.

Jonathan didn't shift his gaze or even blink. "I think it's a little late to be having this conversation. We *are* married, Steph."

Stephanie shook her head slowly, not taking her eyes off of his. "Well, I don't feel married, Jonathan. And when I do, it doesn't feel good."

"What are you trying to say, Stephanie? Did something happen while I was gone? Is it someone else?"

"No, Jonathan," Stephanie said. Her tears were now slowly becoming sobs. "It's nothing like that. I love you very much. It's just . . ."

"Just what? Please, if you love me, you'll tell

me what's going on." Jonathan's eyes were welling with tears as he spoke.

Stephanie wanted nothing more than to rush out of the apartment right then, but she cared about Jonathan too much to do that. Instead, she met his gaze squarely. "I'm still a kid."

Jonathan looked at her sadly.

"I—I guess I just realized that this weekend, Jonathan," she said softly.

Jonathan took her hands in his. "Maybe—maybe we didn't think things through. I just thought we loved each other enough to make things work."

Stephanie shook her head. "It's all my fault. I—I don't know why I was in such a rush."

Jonathan's head sagged. "I was never sure I could make you happy, Steph."

"It's just that I need time to figure out my life," Stephanie tried to explain. "I need to play. I need to have a few more adventures before I can settle down."

Jonathan shook his head. "I have to tell you, Steph. I've been feeling way over my head lately. It's going to be a while before I have enough money to buy a home or the things we need. . . ."

A lump began to form in Stephanie's throat, and she couldn't speak. Jonathan had tried very hard to make her happy. But how could they have taken such a major step without thinking? And what were they going to do now?

CHAPTER 12

The inside of Max Ridgefield's van looked like a recording studio on wheels. Scuffed speakers, mikes, soundboards, and rolls of wire were piled in the back along with overflowing boxes of tapes, stacks of CDs, and an open toolbox with a broken headset hanging out of the top.

"Do you know how many times I've tangoed in broad daylight in the middle of a barn?" Max asked Bess.

Bess laughed as they bumped onto the main highway to head for Weston. It was past noon, and the state police had finally reopened all the roads. "Dozens of times. I could tell."

"Watch this," Max said, reaching forward.

"What?" Bess giggled.

"Are you ready?"

"No!"

"Good." He flicked a makeshift switch above

145

the windshield and the back of Bess's seat began to recline.

Bess laughed out loud. A moment later she was lying on her back, staring at the van's ripped vinyl ceiling. "Planning on taking advantage of me?"

"Advantage? No way," Max replied. He flicked the switch again and Bess was flung forward against her seat belt. Max winced. "Still needs some fine-tuning."

Bess bent over with laughter.

"Here's another feature of the Rockmobile," Max went on, pulling a lever underneath the dashboard. A long tray filled with CDs and tapes glided out. "I like to have music at my fingertips. Take your pick."

"I'm almost afraid to ask what else your van can do," Bess said as she selected some old jazz tunes.

Max gave her a brilliant smile. "Don't ask. I don't want to scare you away." He put on the CD, and cool, mellow tones filled the van.

Bess gazed at the frozen scenery rushing by, and she felt that nothing could scare her away from Max right then. The closer she got to Max Ridgefield, the freer and happier she felt. She forgot all about feeling depressed, fat, and out of control.

"Thanks for coming out to meet me," Max said shyly, taking her hand and squeezing it. "That took guts."

"You're the one with guts, Max," Bess said

shyly. "Remember? You were my secret admirer."

Max reddened. "I didn't know how to ask you out, Bess. You were the star of *Cat on a Hot Tin Roof* with a big Broadway director. I was the lowly sound man."

"I'm glad you got around to it," Bess said gently, squeezing his hand back just as he began to pump the brakes. Up ahead, a long line of idling cars and trucks was forming on the highway. Clouds of steamy exhaust drifted skyward.

"Uh-oh," Max groaned. "We're never going to get back to campus."

Bess saw a uniformed trooper walking up the road, talking to drivers.

"Sorry, folks," the trooper said, when he got to the van. "A vehicle spun out on the bridge up ahead, and I'm afraid we have to wait for the Weston Medic One to arrive before we can move it."

Max turned off the ignition. Then he leaned back, put his hands behind his head, and smiled over at Bess. "Looks like we've been thrown together in the middle of nowhere."

"Mmmmm." Bess undid her seat belt and slid a little closer to Max.

Max slipped an arm around her shoulder and gently pulled her toward him. He touched his lips lightly to hers.

"Max," Bess whispered as she circled her arms around his neck. "I hope that bridge is closed for a very, very long time. . . ."

* * *

"Thanks for the ride," Nancy shouted to the driver of the semi who'd picked up her and Michael in Braemer. They hopped out onto Weston's main drag and waved as the man turned his rig toward the main highway.

"Nice guy," Nancy said as they climbed over a mound of dirty snow left by the city plows. They stepped onto the shoveled sidewalk and headed toward campus. "It was nice of Ollie to hook us up with him."

Michael hitched his camera case higher on his shoulder. "Good old Ollie. The guy deserves a credit at the end of our next broadcast."

Nancy's boots crunched on the snow. "Hope they can tow your car back by tomorrow."

"Yeah, me, too," Michael answered.

Nancy veered around a pile of shoveled snow in front of a store. "At least the engine's in the back of the VW and not the front, where it got smashed in."

Michael cleared his throat uncomfortably. "Uh-huh."

Nancy's eyes darted over to peek at him. She knew that a lot had changed between them in those few hours in the barn, but she didn't know what to say about it. She gazed up at the clock above the ornate entrance gate. "Four o'clock," she said instead. "We have so little time to put the show together."

"Yeah," Michael said. "And we have to track down Ace."

Nancy shrugged. "Even if we do find him, then

what? He doesn't have to tell us anything about the Money Plane. And if we start talking about some guy named Goldfinger, he's likely to laugh in our faces. Why should he talk? He's covered his tracks."

"Why are you so pessimistic all of a sudden?" Michael acted confused. "Do you just want to forget the whole thing?"

"No. I didn't say that," Nancy said. "I'm just trying to be realistic. I really want this show to work."

"Then let's get to Owens Hall and track Ace down." Michael gave her a friendly pat on the back, and it sent chills through Nancy's body.

"It's behind the music building," Nancy said nervously. "Can't we move a little faster? I'm cold."

"I'm dragging a thirty-pound load of equipment here," he said. "If you helped, maybe we'd get there faster."

"I don't believe my ears," Nancy said with a smile. "I think you just asked for my help, tough guy."

"Whatever. Let's just get there," Michael said sheepishly. "It *is* cold out here."

When they reached the broad campus Walk, a winter wonderland spread out before them: cross-country skiers dodged ice sculptures, groups of red-faced students clustered around espresso stands, and armies of snowball-throwers were armed and ready. Owens Hall was a small, modern dorm surrounded by a small concrete plaza that was crisscrossed with bike stands.

"Come on," Nancy called out, trudging past a man shoveling the front entrance walk.

"Hey, Nancy!" She heard a voice calling from up above. "Nancy, up here."

"Jean-Marc?" Nancy shouted. Out of the corner window on the third floor she could see Jean-Marc's head of unruly black hair whipping in the breeze. "What are you doing up there?"

"I need to talk to you," he shouted back. "I've been trying to reach you since yesterday. Wait there."

Nancy glanced at Michael, who was scowling at her with narrowed eyes. "What?" she asked.

"Have you been talking to Jean-Marc behind my back?" Michael snapped.

Nancy's shoulders slumped forward, and she shook her head. "Give it up, Michael. He just saw us walking down here, okay?"

Jean-Marc strode up to them, wearing an unzipped parka over a thin sweatshirt. He was pale. "Thanks for waiting."

Nancy glanced up at his worried face. "Jean-Marc, what's up? We were just about to go into this dorm to find Ace."

Jean-Marc nodded. "He lives here. I live here, too. That's how I met him."

"Before you say anything," Nancy told him, "I have to tell you that we've been investigating the Money Plane for *Headlines*."

"I thought so," Jean-Marc said quietly.

"We've just been over at Brockton College," Michael began. "Are you aware of what happened over there?"

"Yeah, I know," Jean-Marc answered soberly.

"Will you talk to us about it?" Nancy asked.

"Yeah." Jean-Marc looked down at the ground. "I think it's time."

"Let's walk," Nancy said.

"You know," Jean-Marc said in a quiet voice, "I've been wanting to say something to both of you for a while."

Nancy kicked a chunk of snow. "We were pretty pushy with you in the student union after that meeting. We're sorry about that." Surprisingly, she noticed, Michael nodded his agreement.

Jean-Marc put his hands up. "No. I had no right to get all bent out of shape with you. But you see, I was starting to get worried about the game."

"Then why didn't you say anything?" Michael prodded.

Jean-Marc shrugged. "I was scared. I didn't want any exposure. The last thing I need is to get kicked out of Wilder."

"The way the game is set up, a lot of people are bound to lose money," Nancy pointed out. "Including the friends you pulled into the game."

Jean-Marc made a fist. "I just didn't think it through. I wanted the money—I got sucked into it."

"We want to get the word out," Michael said.

"People are dropping money like candy, and only about ten percent of the players will ever see a profit."

"Why did you get involved with the game, Jean-Marc?" Nancy asked as they headed through the glass doors of the student union. The three of them slipped into a corner booth in the coffee shop.

"It was stupid," Jean-Marc said. He rubbed his eyes. "It boiled down to one thing: I had this crazy idea that I had to have a Harley-Davidson. Can you believe that? I'd been saving for two years. But there was no way I was going to get the thousands I needed unless I did something big. . . ."

"Will you help us?" Nancy asked him after a pause. "I don't know if we can put this story together without your help."

Jean-Marc nodded. "I want to do the decent thing. Heaven knows what Holly will think of me if I walk away from this."

"How did you get involved with Ace?" Nancy asked.

"I met him at the beginning of the year," Jean-Marc said quietly. "At a party for transfer and exchange students. We played a little pool. Come to think of it, I don't even know his real name."

"We're pretty sure his name is John O'Rourke," Michael told him.

Jean-Marc sighed. "Anyway, he came up to me one day later and said he had a business proposition called the Money Plane. He came on with this line about how he was looking for outgoing guys like me who'd be good at rounding up investors."

"You weren't suspicious?" Nancy asked, sipping her coffee.

"I should have been," Jean-Marc admitted. "But Ace made it sound like a dream come true, and I really wanted to believe it."

"So he thought you could round up a lot of new players," Michael prompted him.

"Yeah. And he talked a little bit about how it was against school policy, but I was won over by his line about the game being a win-win deal for everyone."

"Did you invest your own money?" Nancy wanted to know.

Jean-Marc shrugged. "Not much. Ace gave me a crew seat on the very first pyramid. So it was free. I rose up to the pilot's seat in just a few days, and collected my twelve hundred dollars without paying a dime."

"Sounds like free money to me," Michael pointed out.

"I turned right around and paid one hundred fifty dollars to join another pyramid," Jean-Marc went on, "and I earned twelve hundred dollars from it at that meeting the other night."

"Wow," Nancy sat back in her chair. "So you cleared two thousand, two hundred fifty dollars in just a few weeks for practically no work."

"Oh, I'm paying for it right now. The campus is swamped with hundreds of 'passengers' trying to recruit new players. And they're all converging on me with their anxieties. I feel terrible."

Michael crossed his arms. "Surely people have to be catching on."

"The game's too risky for any player who doesn't join early enough," Jean-Marc said. "That fact didn't hit me until I heard you work out the math at the union. Now I'm stuck because I talked a lot of people into joining. A *lot* of people."

"Did you talk to Ace about it?" Michael asked.

Jean-Marc shook his head in disgust. "I talked to him yesterday. Told him I thought we should have some controls on this. And some better information for players."

Nancy's eyes opened wide. "What did he say?"

"He laughed."

"That doesn't surprise me," Michael said, rubbing his chin thoughtfully.

"He said it wasn't his problem. Everybody had to take their chances," Jean-Marc said. "The conversation got pretty ugly, so I didn't talk to him long."

"We just talked to a woman at Brockton College who said she was recruited last year by a guy who matches Ace's description," Michael told him. "She said Ace bragged once about a contact of his who was the financial wizard behind his success. She thought Ace referred to him once as his 'Goldfinger.'"

"Could be," Jean-Marc agreed.

"Someone has to be making big money with this," Nancy pointed out, "or the scam wouldn't be so widespread."

Jean-Marc nodded. "I get that feeling, too. I didn't have the impression that Ace was working alone. He's not smart enough for that. But I never asked any questions."

Nancy drew out the tip sheet from her purse. "See this?"

Jean-Marc bent forward.

"I found it on the floor near Ace's sign-up table at the Thayer Hall meeting." Nancy explained. "See? It's a tip sheet for Money Plane recruiters."

"It's initialed, too," Michael pointed out. "G.G. Do you know who that could be?"

Jean-Marc shrugged. "I wish I could help you there, but it doesn't ring a bell. But I'll do what I can to help you expose this thing."

Michael and Nancy looked at each other and knew they were thinking the same thing. They had a plan brewing, and all they had to do now was fine-tune the details.

"Okay, beautiful," Montana said. "Let's put the finishing touches on your lovely nose."

She stood back and squinted at the ice sculpture. A replica of her own face and body stared back at her.

"People always said you were artistic, but slightly cold-hearted," Montana muttered to her ice-self.

She glanced up at the empty windows of Jamison Hall. Then she stepped carefully into the patch of snow in front of the sculpture, which she'd kept untouched.

"First the *I*," Montana muttered, her breath coming out in frosty puffs in the artificial light from the street lamps. "Then the apostrophe-*M*." She drew the letters on the snow with the toe of her boot.

When she was done, she stood back to admire her work, wondering if it would have the slightest effect on Cory.

" 'I'M SORRY.' " She read over the words she'd made in the snow. "I really am, too, Cory."

She sat down on a nearby tree stump and began packing a hard snowball. "Maybe that's why it's so easy for me to crack jokes on the air and kid around about everyone and everything," Montana whispered to herself. "Maybe I do have a heart made of ice."

Montana planted one foot in front of her and threw the snowball as hard as she could at Cory's first-floor window.

A moment later there was movement behind the glass and the grating sound of the window being opened.

When Cory's head appeared, Montana's heart pumped double-time. But all she could do was stand there, her arms hanging at her sides.

For a moment he just stared at the sculpture and the message written in the snow. Wisps of his longish red hair blew in the light breeze, and his blue eyes looked like two cold stormy lakes. Montana bit her lip as he slowly closed the window and disappeared from view.

Montana sat down on a snowy rock and felt the pull of tears. Why *should* Cory forgive her? He was too sensitive and smart for that. The side of her that he'd seen was fickle and thoughtless. She'd blown it.

Through her tears, Montana watched as clumps of snow whooshed off the tree branches. There was the far-off sound of boots crunching through the snow in the gathering dark. It was time for her to dust herself off and go home.

"I'm sorry, too," she heard Cory's voice from the window.

Montana jumped. She jerked her head up and saw Cory's face, now transformed. Smiling, he threw one leg over the windowsill, then the other, and jumped into the soft snow. Montana rushed over to the window.

"You have nothing to be sorry for," Montana said, her eyes searching his. "I was flat-out coming on to Ray, and I hurt you."

Cory shook his head. "He followed you out to your car last night. You didn't ask him, did you?"

"Well, no," Montana faltered. "It's just that . . ."

"Forget it," Cory said softly, slipping his strong arms around her waist and pulling her close. "You tried to talk to me about it this morning— and I took off like a jerk. I didn't even listen."

"Why did you run?" Montana asked, wiping a tear with her sleeve.

Cory turned her toward his dorm and together they began walking arm in arm. He took a deep breath, then let it out slowly. "Because I could see it happening all over again."

Montana stared at him. "What did you see happening?"

Cory bit his lip. "I fall for a girl. Girl sort of falls for me. Girl sees dark, mysterious, moody guy. Girl leaves me for Mr. Mysterious. I'm left holding the bag. In this game, the good guy always finishes last."

Montana stopped him, then cupped his face between her two hands. "I want the good guy, Cory."

Cory's eyes seemed to mist over before he bent down and wrapped her tightly in his arms. "And I want you."

CHAPTER 13

Michael slammed the phone down. "I got Sidney Trenton at home. We're on. We've got permission to use the spy cam."

"Yes," Nancy said, pumping a fist in the air.

Jean-Marc sat stiffly in a chair next to the *Headlines* editing machine.

"What are you guys going to do next?" Jean-Marc wanted to know.

Nancy perched on the edge of her desk in the *Headlines* office. "Our plan is to track down Ace and get him to talk, without knowing he's being taped."

"Yeah, and now we're in business," Michael said hurriedly, reaching for the baseball cap. A tiny wire dangled from the inside of the brim.

"The cap," Nancy explained to Jean-Marc, "is equipped with a small camera. This is what we want you to wear."

Jean-Marc's mouth dropped open. "Cool."

159

Michael showed him the inside of the cap's crown. "We fasten this tiny lens to a hole in the crown of the hat. "That's how we get the video. The microphone's completely hidden, but it does a really good job of picking up voices."

"Now all we have to do is track down Ace and get him to talk," Nancy said anxiously.

"Think you can do it?" Michael gave Jean-Marc a sharp look.

Jean-Marc gave him a thumbs-up sign. "There's a group in Owens Hall that plays pool every Sunday night. Ace is usually there."

"Do whatever you think it'll take to get him to loosen up and talk," Nancy instructed Jean-Marc as they headed back across the campus in the cold, bluish light of dusk. "He needs to trust you."

When the threesome reached Owens Hall, Jean-Marc broke away from Nancy and Michael and hurried through the front doors.

"Go for it," Michael whispered after him. They waited outside a moment.

"Come on," Nancy urged him. "I don't want Jean-Marc to get too far ahead. I want to be right there."

"Jean-Marc said the pool room is in the basement," Michael said quietly. Together, they spotted a staircase leading to the floor below.

Nancy pressed a finger to her lips when they reached the bottom. A dim hallway led to a room in the back. She could hear the distant sound of a cue cracking against a ball.

"Hey, Mr. Cash Flow," they heard a voice sing out. "Buy that Harley yet?"

"Hey, Ace," they heard Jean-Marc respond. "Not yet. But it won't be long now."

"All right" was Ace's reply. Nancy and Michael moved carefully down the passageway, their backs to the wall. "Play a little pool? No one's here yet."

"I'm game," Jean-Marc replied.

Nancy glanced over at Michael. "They're alone."

Michael smiled and gave her a silent thumbs-up.

"Pick your cue, buddy," Ace said. "You break."

Nancy heard the sound of balls cracking against a hard-hit cue ball.

"Nice," Ace said with admiration. "Hey, buddy, you okay? You were pretty worked up about our meeting last night."

"Forget it," Jean-Marc said. "Momentary twinge of guilt, Ace. Tell you what I did. I looked in my wallet, and when I saw all that money, I cooled right down."

Ace laughed. "Oh, man, you're telling me. If folks let themselves be taken—then too bad. It happens every day."

Jean-Marc chuckled. "Except that we're on the receiving end this time, right?"

"No kidding," Ace agreed. "There are lots and lots of desperate suckers on this campus. And it's my aim to milk them for all they're worth."

"Sounds like you have a lot of investing experience, Ace." Jean-Marc began working him. "Was the Money Plane a good way to break into the business?"

"You bet," Ace replied. Nancy heard the cue ball crack again and the sound of a ball plopping into the pocket. Every muscle in her body tensed. She prayed that Jean-Marc could get the information they needed before Ace's pool buddies barged in. "It's giving me the capital I need to break into some other ventures, much to my dad's amazement."

"Your dad?" Jean-Marc prompted.

"Yeah. Mr. Big Shot Corporate Farmer," Ace said with disgust. "Always said I'd never amount to anything, had no business sense—but I'm showing him," Ace went on. "I took in about five grand over at Brockton College last year. This year should be even better."

"You went to Brockton last year?"

There was a pause, and the snap of the cue again. "Yeah, I did. Transferred here after a little spat with the administration."

"Bummer," Jean-Marc remarked. "Red ball, corner pocket."

"Yep. I had a pretty big airplane game over there, but someone complained and the dean fingered me."

"Stupid bureaucrats," Jean-Marc said, egging him on.

"The problem with bureaucrats is that they don't know about business risk," Ace complained. "They make it their mission in life to protect the stupid and innocent. My pal Goldfinger warned me, but I was just temporarily unlucky, I guess."

"Who's Goldfinger?"

"A friend who got me into investments," Ace explained. "He held a meeting at the Valley Inn last year for Brockton students. Turned me on to a number of business opportunities. Slick guy. Very smart. Wears a gold watch that must have set him back a couple of grand."

Nancy gave Michael a quick nod before they rushed into the room and confronted Ace. "You're done cheating students here at Wilder," Nancy told him.

Ace's narrow, freckled face expressed his shock. "What are you talking about?"

Jean-Marc slowly removed his cap. "You're ripping people off on this campus, and we're going to let people know about it."

"Why, you—" Ace shouted, lunging for Jean-Marc. "What've you got there? Some kind of recording device?"

Jean-Marc swiftly handed the hat and connecting wires to Michael, who locked it up in his case.

"That's illegal!" Ace shouted. "Hey, I've got my rights."

Nancy stared him down. "So do all the people you ripped off. Now it's just a matter of showing this to the police, Ace. They'll decide what they want to do with you."

Ace lunged for Jean-Marc again and grabbed him by the front of his shirt.

Just then Nancy heard footsteps coming down the stairs. Someone apparently had heard the arguing, or at least that's what Nancy was praying. Ace had Jean-Marc shoved up against a wall when a group of guys burst into the room.

Oh, no! Nancy thought. They're probably Ace's buddies.

"Hey," one of them shouted, helping Michael pull Ace off Jean-Marc. "Hey, knock it off, Ace. What are you doing?"

"You didn't get arrested at Brockton," Michael said, nearly out of breath, "but it's not going to be so easy here at Wilder."

"Someone finally got the goods on this jerk?" one of the guys holding Ace's arms asked. The newcomers started cheering. "Can't say you didn't have it coming."

Nancy sighed. They weren't Ace's thugs after all.

"Do us a favor and keep Ace here while we call the police," Nancy asked the guys as Ace struggled against them. "And whatever you do, don't let go of him."

"Okay, Dad," Stephanie was saying into the phone. "I'm glad you understand. I'll talk to you later."

Stephanie set down the phone.

"Do you want the toaster oven?" Jonathan

asked sadly. "It was a gift from the menswear department."

"You keep it," Stephanie said.

"How did the call to your dad go?" Jonathan asked. He was slowly separating their small stash of tapes and CDs. It was very late Sunday night, and after hours of talking, Stephanie and Jonathan had decided to divorce. Since their marriage was only a few weeks old, they decided a quick break was best.

"He understood," Stephanie said, tears slipping down her cheeks. "He said he'd made a few mistakes himself in his lifetime."

Jonathan put a hand on Stephanie's shoulder. "I'm glad you talked things over."

Stephanie nodded wordlessly. She had been sure her father would gloat when she phoned a few moments ago to tell him she was splitting with Jonathan. But his reaction had been just the opposite.

"I can't believe it," Stephanie said quietly. "He seemed to really understand."

"I'm glad he's agreed to pay your tuition and room and board payments. I don't want you to drop out, Steph. I want the best in life for you—always."

Stephanie nodded. She was getting her old roommate, Casey, back, too. Tomorrow she'd be back to her old life. Older. Wiser. With a bigger heart and a much steadier head. From now on, she knew the security she was looking for could come only from within. No one—not even Jonathan—could give that to her.

By eleven P.M. the sky was choked with stars and the temperature had dropped to a frigid five degrees. The snow was so cold, it squeaked under Ginny's boots as she headed back to Thayer Hall. After four hours in the library, she was ready to crash.

As she made her way to her dorm, she saw the yellow lights of the rooms beginning to wink out.

Ginny sighed. She was glad she'd taken the time to party over the weekend. Ricky had been fun to hang out with, and the storm had been exciting.

"But I didn't find what I was looking for," Ginny whispered to herself. "And I don't know if I ever will."

As she approached the front entrance, she turned her head ever so slightly. She was used to imagining that she would run into Ray, but the figure approaching her really did look like him.

"Ginny?"

Ginny's heart leaped into her throat. "Ray?"

"Hi," he said, walking toward her, his face serious and his eyes shining.

"Wh—what are you doing here?"

Ray smiled and looked at his watch. "It's eleven o'clock, and you're just coming back from the library."

Ginny hugged her books closer and looked up at the stars. "You know me too well."

"Yeah."

Ginny shivered. "What are you doing?"

"I wanted to talk to you."

Ginny stood there, watching her breath come out in frosty clouds. She hadn't seen Ray for so long. She searched his face for a change. Was he different? Happier? All of a sudden, she wanted to know everything.

"I miss you, Ginny," Ray said in a rush. His dark eyes searched hers in the half-light. "I think about you constantly."

Ginny's knees felt like rubber. "But, Ray . . ."

He stepped forward and grabbed both of her arms. "I know. I know. We had to split up. We've been over this. I needed my music. You needed medical school."

Ginny's eyes smarted. "You couldn't meet me halfway."

Ray's eyes seemed to blaze in the darkness. "I know I wouldn't. I was living in a dream world, Gin. A world where we would write songs together. Where we would go to LA together. Where we would live, eat, and breathe music together."

Ginny's heart was bursting. "Why are you going over all this again, Ray? It's too painful."

"Because I wanted to say that I'm sorry," Ray answered simply. Ginny could barely take it all in. "I've been selfish. Arrogant. Stupid. And I ended up with nothing. I shoved you out of my life and now it's empty."

"Ray, I can't believe this. . . ."

"I love you for wanting to be a doctor," Ray said urgently. "I love you for standing firm for what you wanted. I never should have tried to pressure you."

Ginny could barely breathe. "Ray, what are you saying?"

"I'm saying I want to get back together. I want to work things out. I'm saying that I love you."

Ginny threw her arms around Ray and pressed her cheek against the warm black leather of his jacket. She knew they could work it out. She'd always known it. And right then, in the deepest part of her heart, she knew they were together at last—for good.

"Is this the Brockton Valley Inn?" Nancy was asking over the phone.

An hour before the Weston Police had arrived, and after reviewing the tape, they had booked Ace on securities fraud charges.

"Hello," Nancy said politely. "My name is Nancy Drew, and I'm with Wilder University. We're trying to track down an investment expert with the initials G.G. who held seminars in one of your conference rooms last spring."

"I only work on weekends. Could you please call back on Monday?" the woman on the other end of the line asked.

"I'm sorry to trouble you," Nancy continued, "but it's imperative we contact this man immediately."

"Would you hold a moment while I check the records?"

Nancy's heart speeded up. "Certainly."

Holding the receiver, Nancy leaned over and watched Michael run through their interview tape. Her heart beat double-time. She could hardly wait for *Headlines* to air. After the show, the campus would be in an uproar, but her real hope was that Eileen and the others would somehow get their money refunded.

"Here we are," the woman said, returning to the line. "We only have two conference rooms, so I'm looking through the months of March, April, and May. . . ."

"Thank you," Nancy breathed.

"Initials G.G.," the woman said thoughtfully. "Mmmm. Take Weight Off Sensibly Annual Meeting. West Valley CPA Association. Brockton High School Fashion Show. Oh—here . . ."

"Yes?" Nancy said excitedly.

"Gerry Gacetta Investments," the woman said.

"That's it," Nancy said, trying to control the excitement in her voice. If Gerry Gacetta was actually Goldfinger, they'd be getting to the root of what could be a nationwide rip-off.

"He held a seminar here in April; the topic was Five Easy Steps to a Lifetime of Wealth."

"Oh, of course," Nancy said. "Gerry Gacetta."

"As a matter of fact, I remember Gerry," the woman said, breaking into a laugh. "What a card. Great guy."

"By the way," Nancy said politely, "do you know how we can get hold of Mr. Gacetta?"

"Let me check the computer," the woman said. "Mr. Gacetta may have an account with the Valley Inn Corporation. We have a chain of fifteen hundred hotels throughout the country."

"I see."

"Yes, here we are," the woman said.

Nancy's blood was thumping in her chest. "Do you know where he is?"

"As a matter of fact, he's staying at our Valley Inn in Boulder, Colorado."

"A big university town," Nancy whispered. "Thank you," she added, setting the phone down and letting out a whoop.

CHAPTER 14

The steam from three cappuccinos floated delicately into the air at Java Joe's. Tuesday afternoon classes had finished, and it seemed as if half the student body had headed straight for the coffee shop.

"I almost sent you guys a postcard," Nancy joked, setting the three coffees down on a crowded table. Nancy hadn't talked to her friends since Friday, the first day of the blizzard. "I feel as if I've been away for weeks."

George rolled her eyes. "Where I was holed up, there wasn't exactly mail service, either."

"The National Weather Service said that Weston got four feet of snow in twenty-four hours on the weekend." Nancy shook her head. "Biggest snowfall in ten years. Twenty thousand people were without power and every road in the county was closed."

Bess's eyes were shining. "Max and I didn't mind."

171

Nancy eyed her. "Do you have something to tell us?"

Bess laughed. "What can I say? There's nothing like a blizzard to jump-start your love-life."

George's face was hidden behind her cup for a moment. Then she set it down. "Sounds like you've discovered a pretty wonderful guy, Bess."

Bess's eyes sparkled. "I know it's too early to tell, but . . ."

"Bess," Nancy said excitedly. "What are you saying?"

"I'm saying that I'm completely, totally, head-over-heels, dead-sure, falling-down, cross-my-heart crazy about Max Ridgefield."

George sat back. "Tell us how you really feel, Bess."

Bess laughed. "I can't explain it. It just feels right when I'm with Max. We laugh. We talk. We listen to music. It's a new beginning for me."

Nancy reached over and squeezed her hand. "You go, girl. It sounds hokey, but I am so proud of you."

"Proud?" Bess asked. "I didn't do anything."

"Didn't do anything?" Nancy echoed her words in disbelief. "How can you say that? After all you've been through this year, the big issues you've dealt with: you were almost date-raped our second night in college; your boyfriend died tragically; you struggled with bulimia and started a support group on campus . . ."

"Don't forget being the target of a lunatic terrorist," George interrupted.

"You guys are really depressing me," Bess warned. "What's the point?"

"The point, Bess," Nancy said, smiling lovingly at her friend, "is that after all these things, you let this really sweet guy into your life and you find a way to be happy. Now, how many people could have preserved enough self-esteem to open up to—maybe even to love—anyone after all that? So, Bess Marvin, I am proud of you."

"Likewise, Bess," George chimed in.

"Nancy, you sound like my counselor," Bess joked.

"Well," Nancy said, "then you should listen to her. Or start paying to listen to me."

The three of them cracked up laughing.

Nancy turned her twinkling gaze on George. "Okay, George. It's your turn. Sounds like it wasn't so bad being trapped in the boathouse with an English professor."

For a brief instant, Nancy thought she saw something sentimental flicker across George's face. But George quickly covered it with a laugh. "All I can remember is being cold. Speaking of which, does anyone want more coffee? I need another mocha cappuccino."

Nancy eyed George suspiciously. She was obviously trying to get out of talking about her adventure. "Sure, I'll take another cappuccino. Bess?"

"Make mine decaf," Bess said.

"Right," George said as she escaped to the line at the counter.

"What's with George?" Nancy asked, leaning over to whisper. "Do you know something I don't?"

Bess leaned back to get a good look at her cousin standing in line. "I know what you mean. Every time I've brought up the night of the storm, George gets all quiet and very un-George-like."

"Oh, no." Nancy cringed. "I sure hope nothing happened."

"What do you mean, Nancy?" Bess asked very seriously. "Are you thinking something like my second night here?"

Nancy nodded, glancing toward George.

"No, she'd tell us," Bess said.

"I'm going to make sure," Nancy volunteered.

George felt relieved to be standing in line away from Nancy's and Bess's questions. But she also felt guilty for being afraid to share her problem with them. They were her best friends, after all.

The rush at Java Joe's had calmed down since they'd first gotten there. The tables were still mostly full, but no one was waiting for a seat and the line was moving pretty quickly.

"Three capps to stay," George told the woman behind the counter. "One mocha, one decaf, and one regular." When the counter clerk came back with the coffees, George handed her the money.

George set the coffees down on their table.

Nancy looked at Bess before focusing her closest scrutiny on George.

George felt Nancy's detective gaze probing her. "What? What did I do?"

"That's what we want to know," Nancy said gravely. "We want to know if that professor hurt you in the boathouse."

George couldn't believe what she was hearing. "Ross? Are you kidding?"

"No," Nancy replied. "We aren't kidding. You've been so mysterious about that night. There you were with this year's number one hunk all night, and I don't think you've said more than five words about it."

Before George could defend herself, Bess started in. "So it crossed our minds that he might have hurt you—raped you—and that you were too ashamed to tell us."

"Whoa, hold on." George felt a surge of anger rush through her body. "Where do you get off with wondering that? First of all, if I'd been raped, I would have reported it instantly. Second, you don't know anything about Ross Yaeger!"

"George," Nancy said softly. "That's precisely why we're asking. We don't know anything about him, and you won't tell us anything about that night, which isn't like you. So we're left to imagine the worst. Want to set us straight?"

You bet I do, thought George. She turned her coffee cup around and around while staring at it. She was so confused! How could she tell Nancy and Bess that she might be in love with Ross and not with Will? What will they think? Yeah, but what do they think now?

"Okay, okay," George said with a heavy sigh. She took a sip of coffee and noticed how instantly Nancy and Bess had relaxed. *What was I thinking? These are Nancy and Bess. My oldest and dearest friends. I should have been pounding on their doors as soon as I got back.*

"Promise you won't tell a soul," George said.

"Promise."

"Promise."

All three girls leaned forward. They looked as they had so many times in the past, hunched over together, trading secrets.

"Ross wouldn't rape me, or anyone," George began. "The very idea is so absurd that I couldn't believe you were asking."

"You seem to know him very well," Bess commented.

"Yes," George answered. "I do. Ross is the kindest, gentlest, most intelligent man—"

"Ahem." Nancy cleared her throat to get George's attention. "Maybe you should tell us what happened, from the beginning."

"Yeah, that makes sense." George drank some more coffee and began. She told them about being out in the storm and finding the boathouse; how Ross had rubbed warmth back into her hands and spread out his one blanket for the two of them. She told them how they'd talked and talked; she repeated his jokes, which sent Bess and Nancy into howling fits of laughter. And she finished with the morning, when the sun was bright and the sky was clear.

"What about Will?" Nancy asked gently.

"That's right—what about Will?" George covered her eyes. Behind them she could see his face, hear him laughing, remember his gentle loving.

Nancy and Bess held a collective breath.

"I don't know," George said, uncovering her eyes. "I honestly don't know. I love Will, I know I do, but I think I love Ross, too."

The table fell silent.

Nancy finally broke the silence. George knew she would, and she knew what Nancy would ask.

"What about the fact that he's a professor and you're a student, George? A freshman."

"The funny thing, Nancy, is that I don't know Professor Yaeger. I've never met him. It's Ross I know and Ross I was stranded with. It's just plain Ross I may be falling in love with."

"You don't think that's just a way of dodging the issue?" Bess asked.

"It could be, but if it is, I'm fooling myself as well as him. And I think we're both too smart for that."

"Does Will know?" Nancy asked.

"No, there's nothing to know—yet," George said somewhat defensively. "I haven't told Ross how I feel either because I just don't know."

Nancy was puzzled.

"I mean, I do know, but I don't know, you know?" George tried to explain.

Nancy smiled but shook her head. "But don't

you think it would only be fair to talk to Will? You've been together for a while now."

Now angry, George snapped at Nancy. "You don't have to lecture me!"

"George," Bess said, intervening. "I don't think Nancy was lecturing you. She was just stating what is plain to her and me."

George didn't know whether to laugh or cry. Friends could be so irritating and so right.

George wound up smiling. "Okay, okay," she said. "Guilty as charged. So I'll make a confession and then I don't want to talk about it anymore. Agreed?"

Bess and Nancy nodded.

"Not anymore *tonight*," Nancy added.

George laughed. "Deal. I confess that I think I am in love with Ross Yaeger. I confess that I haven't told Will Blackfeather. I confess that I think I love Will Blackfeather. I confess I am a freshman in college, so I am too young to know the answers, but I'm just the right age to have all the questions."

"Bravo, bravo!" Nancy and Bess cried.

The three friends raised their glasses and toasted being freshmen in college.

Another silence descended. George and Bess exchanged glances and turned toward Nancy.

"What?" Nancy asked. "Oh, no, not me."

"Why *not* you?" George and Bess asked in unison.

The three of them were talking as they had in the old days, before college. They hadn't come this close to sharing since coming to Wilder. Who am I to hold out? Nancy thought.

"Okay, I'm ready," Nancy declared. "But first, I want to say that you're the best friends I'll ever have."

Not surprisingly, a few tears came to a few eyes as hands reached out and grasped hands.

"Enough of this sentimental truth and beauty," George said. "On with the nitty-gritty details. Ms. Drew, do you swear to tell the truth, the whole truth, and nothing but the truth?"

"I do."

"State your activities the night of the afore-mentioned blizzard," Bess demanded.

"Short and sweet, guys," Nancy said. Inside, she wondered if she could pull this off. When she stood up and left Java Joe's, would she still have two such wonderful friends? "Here it goes. You know about the car crash and that we spent the night together in the barn."

"Yeah, yeah," George said. "What I don't know is why you aren't in a cast and why Michael Gianelli doesn't have his eyes scratched out."

"That's because on the night of the aforemen-tioned blizzard, stuck in the aforementioned barn with the aforementioned Michael Gianelli—"

"Hold it," George said. Nancy held her breath. "Bess, do you think we're being stalled?"

"There must be some punishment for this," Bess responded.

Nancy let out her deep breath and blurted out, "I fell in love."

After some more shocked silence, George finally asked, "With whom? Were there stray cats, perhaps?"

"You!" Nancy swatted George's arm. "You're so cruel. I fell in love with Michael Gianelli. The only thing you don't know about my night now is that, when I woke up the next morning in the barn, Michael was about to kiss me. Only I freaked and yelled at him. Since then—well, let's just say I made a mistake that I plan to rectify just as soon as we're done spilling our guts."

"Wow," George said. "I don't know what to say, Nan."

"What do you mean?" Bess asked. "That's great, Nancy. Congratulations. On the scale of, say, Peter to Ned, where do you think Michael falls?"

"Hmm," Nancy thought out loud. "Somewhere around, well, around Michael."

"Cheater," Bess grumped.

"Enough, enough," Nancy cried. "No more deep hidden secrets for tonight. Let's leave something to talk about in our old age."

The girls laughed and laughed, getting punch-drunk on their laughter.

An hour later the friends had ordered another round of cappuccinos and were still talking.

"Your *Headlines* broadcast last night was definitely *not* boring," George commented. "That Money Plane game was a full-scale fleecing operation, Nan. Everyone's talking about it."

Bess nodded. "Eileen hasn't stepped out of her room since your show aired, she's so embarrassed."

"That's part of the problem," Nancy said. "Only the winners talked. Everyone else was too humiliated. No one complained."

George made a face. "I could have punched out that Ace when I saw the smirk on his face— bragging about his scam as if he were some kind of financial wizard."

"John O'Rourke," Nancy said. "What a loser."

"The spy cam interview was cool," Bess agreed. "You nailed him."

Nancy flashed a smile. "Believe, me, that felt very good. The police went nuts when they saw the tape. And since it's Ace's second offense, he's getting more than just a slap on the wrist."

George whistled. "What will happen to him?"

Nancy counted out his penalties on her fingers. "He's been kicked out of school. He's been slammed with a huge fine for violating the state's securities fraud laws. And he'll have to spend time in jail."

Bess raised her eyebrows. "And what about Goldfinger? Did the police catch up with him?"

Nancy drank the last of her coffee and nodded. "The Weston Police were great. They tipped off FBI agents in Boulder, Colorado, where the motel agent said he was staying. All they had to do was knock on his motel door and arrest him."

George set down her cup. "Just like that?"

"The feds had been trying to catch up with this

guy for the past year, but he's been slippery," Nancy explained.

"I bet—with all those crazy code names and secret cash payments," George said.

"The guy never actually used his real name during the seminars," Nancy explained. "So no one could pin him down. And his scam was to move around a lot, hitting university towns, where there was always a fresh crop of hungry students."

Bess winced. "And college students aren't always rocket scientists when it comes to money."

"You got it," Nancy agreed. "Economics 101 doesn't always gel with the best of us. No ninety percent of the players lose their money and become the great silent majority."

"Whew," George said.

"It turns out that this Gerry Gacetta would set up at least a half-dozen pilots on each campus for an initial payment of six hundred dollars, with the promise that they'd be assured a co-pilot seat right at the beginning of the game. Gacetta would take his thirty-six hundred dollars and move on to the next town. Meanwhile, the pilot would recoup his six hundred dollars almost immediately when he collected twelve hundred dollars from the first eight passengers."

"Plus a second twelve hundred dollars once he moved up to pilot," George thought out loud. "What a scam."

"When he was moving fast," Nancy explained, "Goldfinger could take in twenty-five thousand dollars in a week. It all adds up. One big winner financed by hundreds of smaller losers."

"What's going to happen to Jean-Marc?" Bess asked nervously. "Holly's a wreck. A lot of Kappas trusted Jean-Marc. I mean, he's Holly's boyfriend. Everyone was sure he was trustworthy."

Nancy nodded. "I think he is, Bess. We couldn't have told our story without him. He told us everything. He filmed Ace with the spy cam, and he's cooperated completely with the authorities."

"Doesn't he get in any kind of trouble?" George asked.

"He found out this afternoon that he'll have to do community service and donate the money he won to charity," Nancy explained.

"I hadn't heard that," Bess said. "Is he getting kicked out of Wilder?"

"No—thank goodness," Nancy replied. "He's basically a good guy who just got swept away by the lure of money."

"You mean *greed*," George threw in.

"Yeah, greed." Nancy nodded. "But I don't think he should miss out on an education because of that."

"I'm taking off," George told Bess and Nancy a few minutes later. "Calculus quiz tomorrow and a paper due Friday."

"Careful out there," Bess called after her.

" 'Bye." George waved, zipping up her jacket and stomping out onto the snowy campus path.

It hadn't been easy talking with Nancy and Bess about Ross Yaeger, she thought as she walked down the shoveled sidewalk. But I'm so glad I did. Now I just have to figure out what I'm going to do. I just have to figure out whom I love.

George suddenly realized how tired she was. Dead tired, thinking about how wonderful both Ross and Will Blackfeather were.

She felt light-headed, as if the sun were shining in her eyes, although winter's night had fallen. But despite her fatigue, she smiled happily at the shadowy, snowy scene. Strange how the snowstorm had changed everything. Ordinary buildings had become spun-sugar castles. The pathways had become silver ribbons, and her heart had been turned upside down.

Why am I such an idiot? she asked herself. Here I am, in love with the most gorgeous, intelligent, loving guy—Will Blackfeather.

So what was it about Ross Yaeger that had found its way into her heart? How was he able to know her so well in such a short time? Why couldn't she just forget him? Or why couldn't she forget Will?

Suddenly George stopped in her tracks, causing a group of students behind her to bump into her. Oh, no! She let out a moan. I'm never going to forget either one of them.

The snowy outline of Jamison Hall shimmered in the night ahead, and George hurried to get up to her room where she could think. Before she got far, however, she caught a movement out of the corner of her eye that was different from all the other movement around her. She turned to focus on what it was.

"Ross?" she whispered.

They hadn't seen each other since the boathouse. Instead of ski clothes, his trim body was clad in corduroys and a brown leather bomber jacket.

But she couldn't have missed him. He was standing stock-still on the steps of Graves Hall, staring at her. Students were flowing around him, from building to path to dorm, but his eyes remained fixed on her.

"George!" she heard him shout, and saw him approach. Her first instinct was to run, but her legs wouldn't move.

"George," Ross said. His blue eyes were shining. He paused, as if not knowing what to say. "How are you—getting along?"

"Fine."

Ross just stood there, reading her face as if it were a favorite book he'd read and reread all his life.

"How are you?"

"I'm good."

"No frostbite?"

"Nope. Just a little tired still. But—" George closed her mouth as she searched his face for an answer.

Ross's expression became serious. "I need to see you again."

George started to say no but found herself repeating his words. "I need to see you again, too."

Ross smiled like a little boy. "I think about you all the time, George."

George stared down at her boots in the snow. The snow that changed everything. "I think about you *and* Will all the time."

Ross raked his hair back with a hand. "I—I don't know what to say, George. There are so many unwritten rules: about faculty and students, about old love and new, but I can't let you slip away."

George took a breath. "I may still slip away."

Ross caught her eye and held it before she could turn aside. "I'm scared, too, George."

"You're crazy."

"That, too. I'm going to be at the boathouse tomorrow night at eight," Ross said firmly. "Will you be there?"

George's lower lip began to tremble. "I'm confused, Ross."

"Please be there, George. You're not in this alone. My first promise to you is that we will sort it out. You can't figure out by yourself in a few nights what the poets have been writing about for centuries. Please," Ross said softly, "don't try to do this by yourself. I'll be there tomorrow night. If you don't come, I'll never bother you again." Ross turned to walk away, but George caught his arm.

"I'll be there," she said. A light flurry of snow began to fall.

Ross took her hands and held them as they peered into each others' eyes. "Until tomorrow,"

Ross said quietly before walking away into the white-speckled night.

"See you later, Nan," Bess called as the two parted company outside. Bess rushed off to a Kappa meeting. For once Nancy didn't feel she had to rush anywhere.

The Money Plane was history. She didn't have an unreasonable amount of homework, and suddenly she felt like doing something other than going back to her room and cracking open a book.

She stared around the darkened campus, feeling the freedom to choose any direction. Nancy decided it was her turn to enjoy the snow.

She found herself walking toward the lake. The path had been plowed around it and there was no more snow in the forecast for days, so she felt secure making the trek.

The moon shone in a brilliant, fingernail crescent that reminded Nancy how such beauty, as well as damaging storms, was part of the universe she inhabited.

The snow-covered lake spread out pristinely before her. The forest sounds were muffled by the insulating snow. Creatures were hibernating. Nancy felt at peace with the world.

As she approached the boathouse, she wondered what George would decide to do, which made her think again about what Bess had been through.

Nancy sat on a stack of logs outside the building and stared out over the flat expanse of snowy lake.

"Hello." Her peacefulness was interrupted by a voice.

"Not another word," she commanded. She sat for a moment without taking her eyes off the lake, then rose to face the guy she had heard following her. "Don't move," she told him.

He stood as still as possible, but he started to speak.

"What did I just say?" Nancy asked.

The guy shut up and lowered his head.

Nancy walked one full circle around him before stopping in front of him. She took his face in her hands and lifted it so she could see his liquid brown eyes. He seemed about to speak, so she lay her finger on his mouth. "Shhhhh."

She raised her right arm and put it on his left shoulder and raised her left arm to his right shoulder. Nancy allowed the man to close his arms around her back as she wrapped her hands around his neck.

Nancy smiled into his face as broadly as his smile fell on hers. She reached up with her whole body and gave Michael Gianelli a warm, deep, passionate, and loving kiss.